The Wrathful Mountains

Tales from Nōl'Deron

Lana Axe

AxeLord Publications
ISBN-10: 0692581715
ISBN-13: 978-0692581711

Cover art by Michael Gauss

For my sisters.

Chapter 1

Annin slumped back against the mattress, her muscles aching from exertion. Too many hours had passed, and the baby had not come. Like too many others, this child was doomed. A mixture of despair and grief plagued the young mother's heart, and she wept for the daughter that she would never meet.

Cradling her sister's head in her arms, Tashi whispered, "You must hold on, Annin." Their own mother had died giving birth to Annin, and Tashi feared she would lose her sister the same way.

"It can wait no longer," the doula said, wiping blood from her hands. "I must remove the baby or both mother and child will die." Her dark eyes stared at Tashi, daring her to refuse.

As High Priestess of the Ulihi tribe, Tashi had final say in all matters of the body. The doula could not proceed without permission, otherwise she risked unleashing a plague of evil upon the tribe. Glancing down at her sister, Tashi knew what had to be done.

Gently placing Annin's head upon her pillow, Tashi jumped to her feet. Stepping outside the birthing hut, she dashed through the village center to her own hut. A flame burned brightly at the center of the one-room dwelling, and Tashi paused before it. The image of her mother, her ebony skin glistening in the firelight, stood before the priestess. Flames replaced her once-raven-black hair, but her black eyes stared knowingly at her daughter. A mirror image of her mother, Tashi looked upon this face with regularity. The image in the flames did not unnerve her, nor did it give her cause for concern. "She will not go with you today," she stated. The image vanished, leaving behind no trace of its sudden appearance.

Her eyes scanned the piles of bones and sacred stones that littered the numerous tables of her hut. The tools of her trade, a High Priestess was charged with the care of her tribe's most prized possessions. Many of these items were irreplaceable, thanks to the dwarves who had taken the tribal lands away from her people. Tashi did not care. She tore through the items like a whirlwind, knocking many of them to the dirt floor. Hidden beneath a stack of dyed furs lay a dagger of obsidian. Clutching the blade in her hand, Tashi returned to the fire.

Extending the dagger over the flames, she spoke an incantation. "*Weevodo kee-uma,*" she repeated, her eyes fixated on the blade. Its edges glowed orange, but still she held it to the fire. "*Errda kee-omo,*" she said as she flipped the blade over. The fire sputtered, sending a rain of orange sparks over the priestess's head. With a fluid motion, she lifted the blade high, casting her gaze to the small opening at the top of her hut. The moon shone down upon her, lending its silver rays to the black blade. "*Lu-omo, kee-vodo!*" Tashi shouted to the night. Hugging the hot blade to her breast, she darted from her home.

All was silent as the ebony-skinned priestess stepped inside the birthing hut. Her heart raced as she scanned the interior, her senses on high alert. Every step felt like an eternity as she moved closer to the curtain that separated her sister from the hut's entrance. Gripping the dagger tighter, she reached for the curtain and peeled it back. Annin lay unmoving upon her bed.

"Does she live?" Tashi asked, her voice thin.

"Barely," the doula answered, snatching the knife away. She returned to the motionless girl and lifted the sheet from her belly.

Tashi moved to her sister's side, once again cradling her head in her arms. Annin's eyes fluttered slightly, proving that she still had breath in her lungs. Tashi closed her eyes, imploring the gods not to take her sister this night.

Combing her fingers through Annin's soft curls, Tashi whispered, "Stay with me."

From the herb pouch on her hip she retrieved a small pot of medicine. Annin winced as her sister rubbed the foul-smelling substance onto her gums, but she had not the strength to protest.

"It will dull your pain," Tashi promised.

The doula took a deep breath before positioning the blade against the young mother's abdomen. Whispering a prayer to the gods, she slid the knife over Annin's skin, creating a passageway for the struggling child. Tashi closed her eyes to the sight of her sister's blood. Squeezing the girl's hand, she muttered an incantation, imploring the gods to preserve the life of both mother and child.

Despite her lack of recent experience, the doula's hand moved steadily as she lengthened the cut. Setting the knife aside, she reached in to retrieve the child. The mother showed no sign of pain, and the child did not move. As she removed the infant girl from her mother, the doula's heart sank. The child was blue. She immediately began clearing the child's airway, but still she drew no breath.

"I've waited too long," the doula said, clutching the child to her breast.

Tashi moved away from her sister and approached the doula, a savage look gleaming in her dark eyes. "Give her to me," she demanded.

Hesitating a moment, the doula handed the child to the priestess. Tashi grabbed the child by her legs, holding her upside down with one hand. Stepping through the curtain, she exited the hut and held the child high, calling upon the Moon Goddess. "Shine your light upon this child," she pleaded. "Do not take another from us." For the past ten years, no child of the Ulihi tribe had survived infancy. Most were stillborn, and too many mothers were lost in the process. Despite all of Tashi's efforts beseeching the gods for their blessings, the situation had not improved. Now her own sister and niece hung in the balance. It was too much to bear.

Seeing no change in the child, Tashi spit on the ground. "You are no Goddess," she shouted to the moon. Darting back inside the hut, she grabbed a woolen blanket and swaddled the child. Rubbing vigorously against the child's chest, she implored her to breathe. "Just one breath, Little One," she whispered. Turning her over, she smacked the child's back, doubting it would do any good. The doula had already tried everything.

"Your sister is dying," the doula said.

Tashi did not hear the woman approach, and startled at her words. Turning sharply, she said, "You will save this child." Thrusting the child into the doula's arms, she focused her attention on her sister. "I will not let this happen," she said, squeezing the girl's hand. Annin's face grew pale, her breathing barely perceptible. Tears splashed on her sister's forehead as Tashi leaned in to kiss her.

A gentle cry sounded behind the curtain, and Tashi's heart nearly stopped. Walking toward her was the doula, her face beaming.

"The child lives," the woman said.

Tashi stood and looked down at her niece, so fragile, so small. No power of this world or the next would take this child from her. She would live and grow under the watchful eyes of Annin and Tashi. She would become the next High Priestess, or there would never be another. The tribe was too small, the lack of children reducing their number to near extinction. "Our people will survive," she said to the child. "You are our future, our hope." Gently she kissed the girl's forehead. "Give her to her mother," she told the doula.

"But she is too weak to feed her," the doula protested.

"Prepare some goat's milk for her," Tashi replied. "And give Annin some as well. She must keep her strength."

The doula nodded once, but her eyes betrayed her true feelings. She did not expect Annin to survive, and the child was weak. Neither of them were likely to live out the night, but she would not disobey the priestess's orders.

Looking to her sister, Tashi said, "The gods be damned. I will save you." Glancing at the baby, she added, "Both of you."

Once more Tashi stepped out into the darkness, bound for her own hut. At three hours past midnight, there were no other villagers about, no one to witness what she was about to do. Cold and still, the night alone would bear witness to her transgression.

Her steps heavy, she made her way back to her hut, the fire reflected in her eyes. On a low shelf sat dozens of clay and wood statues, all depicting the female form. These were fertility symbols, sacred to her tribe. Some had been crafted centuries earlier, when her people reproduced with ease and reared healthy children to adulthood. Those days were long gone.

Lifting an idol in her hand, she turned it toward the light. A wide smile stretched across its clay face, its belly round and full. In a swift motion, Tashi threw the idol into the fire, smashing it against the burning logs. Statue after statue followed suit as she screamed to the night. "No more will you mock my people!" Her voice harsh with anger, she cursed the gods who had forsaken the children of her tribe. "You are no longer gods," she said as she tossed the last of the idols into the flames. Falling to her knees, she covered her eyes and wept.

After several moments, Tashi finally looked up, fixated on the scene before her. The destruction of a sacred object was known to invite evil into one's home. As High Priestess, she was expected to protect these items with her life. But Tashi did not regret her actions. In her mind flashed images of dead children, infants who would never know the love of their mothers. All of them she had offered to the gods, their tiny remains bundled and burned, returning to the gods who had sent them to this world. Never would they return. Tashi's heart ached from the loss.

Guilt crept into her soul as she remembered the eyes of grieving mothers, women whom she had instructed to trust in the will of the gods. All of them had done so, believing Tashi to hold the power to converse with these holy beings. Looking to the ground, she admitted to herself that she had no such gift. Her entire life was a lie, as were the lives of all priestesses before her. They held no power; they could not sway the gods in anyone's favor. Still her tribe believed, despite decades of failure. Had there ever been a priestess who could truly converse with the gods? Did the gods even care what a woman had to say? Tashi shook her head. "There are no gods," she whispered to the fire.

Lying back on the dirt floor, Tashi tried to calm her mind. The tiny cry of Annin's daughter echoed in her ears. *The child must survive at any cost,* she decided. *I cannot sway nonexistent gods, but I can awaken the darkness.*

Dark magic was forbidden among the Ulihi. It was widely believed the use of such spells were responsible for the downfall of her people, that they had been punished for summoning dark spirits and requesting their favors. But if the gods did not exist, who would punish Tashi for her actions? Everything had been a lie. Perhaps the dark spirits did not exist either. The priestess decided to find out.

On the far wall of her hut hung a series of ritual masks, each placed precisely according to the constellation it embodied. The heavens themselves were represented, each deity's face looking upon the priestess. One mask beckoned to her, the one representing a long-dead god. He had slept for millennia, banished to the center of the mountain, never again allowed to roam free. His crimes against the benevolent gods earned him this punishment, and to call upon him could unleash a plague of evil upon the world.

Tashi strode to the wall and looked upon the mahogany mask, its surface cracked and lined with age. It bore the likeness of the dead god, his grim expression a warning to all who dared worship him. "You do not scare me," Tashi said, reaching for the mask. "There can be no evil if there is no good." The other gods were deaf to her pleas, they cared not for her people. Perhaps this one would take action.

"Darkness take me," the priestess said as she placed the mask upon her face. "My life for my sister, my life for my niece." With careful steps she approached the fire and began to dance. Chanting the words she had learned as a child, she summoned the dead god to aid her. These words were forbidden, and she had been warned against using them. Her grandmother had beaten her after that lesson simply to drive home the message. This was not to be taken lightly.

Raising and lowering her arms, Tashi imitated the movements of the Night Heron. Slow and methodical, she praised the graceful bird, all the while continuing her song. Her dance became wilder as she worked herself into a frenzy, the birdlike movements becoming those of the She-Cat. Her voice crying out to the night, she pounced and leapt with the grace of the predator. Slowing once more, she stalked the flames as if they were her prey.

Within the flame something awoke, the eyes of Tashi's mother flashing a warning. Tashi leaned close, defying the apparition, the dead god's mask grinning in reply. Her mother's eyes vanished, leaving the priestess alone with the flames.

The chant went on for hours, her voice changing from soft to booming, smooth to shrill. A series of different creatures joined the dance, the priestess summoning all their spirits to assist in calling the dark deity. More and more voices joined her own, each imploring the ancient spirit to waken.

Nearly exhausted, Tashi continued, her sister's life hanging in the balance. If she stopped before the dead god answered, there would be no hope. If he still existed, she must wake him. There was no other way.

As the stars faded from the sky, Tashi collapsed. The fire burned low, nearly suffocated by the presence of so many spirits. The dead god had not answered, and Tashi could do no more. Lying on her side, she wept, her tears falling upon the earth. Her heart cried out for the sister she would lose, and the child who would not live to know her. Was the dead god as useless as all the others? Tashi feared the answer.

As she lay motionless, the ground beneath her rumbled, stirring her from her rest. Wood and clay items rattled on her shelves, some of them falling to the ground. Still the earth continued to quake. Stumbling to her feet, the priestess swallowed hard. A loud groan sounded beneath her, the presence of evil was near.

Somewhere deep in the mountain, an ancient mind began to stir.

Chapter 2

High in the mountains, Kaiya stood with her eyes tightly shut, her arms outstretched. Silver magic danced upon the palms of her hands, while her violet locks swayed with the breeze. This was one of a choice few places where the dwarf woman could find peace and meditate with the wind as her guide.

The silence of the mountain caressed her, her skin tingling in response. Magic washed over her, the element of air surrounding her body and filling her lungs. The soft fragrance of mountain pine wafted to her nostrils, reminding her she was at home. Here in the Wrathful Mountains was where she belonged.

Kaiya's mind drifted from village to village, from lower in the mountains to the king's throne farther north, and on to the very summit. Snow blanketed the farthest reaches, concealing a mind that she had not sensed before. Curious, she focused her magic to investigate it, but the presence was fleeting, disappearing into the depths. Whatever it was, it had no desire to communicate with the sorceress.

Opening her gray eyes, Kaiya witnessed the setting of the sun. A twinge of fear ran down her spine. Something was hiding its thoughts from her. Something didn't want to be seen. Standing tall, the sorceress showed no sign of her anxiety. What did this creature have to hide? Did it simply desire privacy, or did it fear her? *Do not provoke me,* she projected with her mind. Whatever it was, it needed to know that she would stand to protect her people, and she was not to be crossed.

Wrapping herself in her woolen cloak, she turned her thoughts to the impending darkness. The first stars appeared in the sky, the sun's orange fire disappearing on the horizon. Perfecting her circular arrangement of stones, she closed her eyes and focused her magic to the south wind. Pulling its heat through her body, she placed a hand upon the stones, spreading silver magic across their surfaces. A fire roared to life—yellow at first, then deepening to red.

Hours of meditation left Kaiya unable to sleep. She lay back, looking up at the stars. Silver windows into the past shone down upon her, their secrets stretching back to eternity. What had their eyes seen? Reaching out with her magic, the sorceress attempted to find out. No matter how hard she tried, they remained elusive, refusing to allow her entrance into their consciousness. They held fast to the void, defying all worldly magic. *Someday…* she thought to herself.

This wasn't the first time Kaiya had attempted magic beyond her abilities. Growing up with no magical being to guide her forced her to push her own limits. There was no one to tell her she couldn't.

Dwarves were not known for their magical talents. With the rare exception of metalsmiths who could carve the ancient runes, no dwarf practiced any sort of magic. Kaiya was born different. She had a natural affinity for the element of air, and it had shaped her entire life.

For many years, Kaiya was an outcast among her kind. They thought of her as a witch, one who would cast evil magic upon them should they allow her to live among them. Unconcerned, Kaiya had pursued her magical studies on her own, learning from the wind itself. She was content to live with her parents in their country home, tending to the sheep and playing with her dogs.

The thought of her beloved mother and father brought a tear to her eye, as did the thought of the dogs she loved as her own children. All would perish in time, but Kaiya would remain. Her magic was a gift, one that imbued her with the power of the Ancients, blessing her with the gift of long life. She would live thousands of years, until she chose to leave this world. Assuming, of course, she was not killed by some other means. Disease and age could not harm her, and mundane weapons were no match for her skills, even if she were attacked while sleeping. Only magic posed any sort of threat, but there was little of that to encounter in the mountains. At least that's what she'd come to believe.

Kaiya had grown complacent over the years. She practiced her skills daily, always eager to learn new spells and perfect the ones she already knew. But there were no troubles in her homeland that required her special attentions. For that, she would have to travel the world, an ambition she held onto for another day. Until her parents were gone, she had no desire to leave the mountains. Unless, of course, she was summoned. Her elven friends in the Vale below might require her assistance, and she would go happily. But beyond that, she hoped not to travel away from the mountains. There would be many years ahead and plenty of time to see the world. For now, she was content staying close to home.

Over the years, most dwarves had come to look on Kaiya with respect. Some still had their reservations, but she had proved herself helpful on many occasions. Her magic could help bring much-needed rain for their crops, and she had been of great assistance when a magical plague descended on a nearby village. Word had spread of her talents, and she'd even had the pleasure of an audience with the king. Not that Kaiya cared much for royalty. Politics didn't interest her in the slightest, and she had no desire to join the ruling family.

As the moon made its path across the sky, sleep still eluded the sorceress. She could not forget about the presence she sensed in the mountain, a nagging feeling ever creeping into her mind. Refusing to stand back up and try reaching out to it, she forced herself to remain on the ground. *I have to get at least a few hours' sleep*, she told herself. Drawing energy from the air, she channeled her magic throughout her body, encasing herself in a soft, white glow. Within minutes the glow subsided, and the sorceress fell asleep.

A hazy vision of her parents' farm played out before her eyes. Two of her brothers tended the flock, having returned home to aid their ailing father. Kaiya watched idly from her seat beneath an oak tree, leaning against its wide trunk. Lazily she turned a sphere of silver magic over in her fingers, its light dancing upon her skin. Turning her gaze toward the mountain's summit, she glimpsed a darkened figure, its arms spread wide to the sky. As she pondered who this person might be, it sank back into the depths, disappearing within the rocks.

Before her eyes, the farmhouse disappeared, and she found herself standing high in the mountains, her feet buried deep in snow. A wild wind blew around her, but it carried no snowflakes nor the frigid chill of a mountain winter. Instead, tiny pebbles drifted on the breeze, pelting her face and forcing her to shield her eyes. Again a dark figure appeared in the distance, but as she stepped forward to approach it, it sank into the stone.

Kaiya looked up to the stars, but there was only darkness. A layer of dust and clouds hid the light of the heavens from her view, and she strained her eyes to see past it. Reaching out with magic, she felt only emptiness, and a chill ran through her body. The ground beneath her feet groaned, a rumble becoming louder and more intense as it continued. Without warning, the ground gave way, a deep chasm opening in the mountain.

Down she fell, grasping desperately at the edge of the rift. It was a futile effort. Her fingers found only loose rock, and she slid, her breath stolen away in a single gasp. Instinctively she called upon the wind, attempting to bend it to her will. But she found nothing. There was no wind, only stillness.

A sense of panic overcame the dwarf woman, her mind racing with spells she could not cast. How could this happen? How could her magic fail her? She should be floating upward on the air, not plunging deep inside the earth.

Crying out, Kaiya tried to call upon the air, but her voice would not project. Instead, she heard nothing but the beating of her own heart, thumping wildly as she continued to fall. Dizziness came over her, the air escaping her lungs. All around her was darkness, the mountain itself closing in on her. Bracing herself for what she might see, she turned her eyes downward to peer into the abyss. Below was only more darkness.

Never one to give up, the sorceress continued to call upon her magic. Perhaps she could force the air into this forbidden space. Pulling at the magic stored inside her, she felt herself weakening, as if something were draining her powers, feasting on her life force. Steeling her mind, she refused to be prey to the unseen entity. There had to be a way out of this.

As she fell deeper into the crevice, the rumbling grew louder. The walls trembled, shaking loose bits of rock and dust that coated her face. Clawing at her face to wipe the dirt away, she felt herself suffocating, buried alive within the rubble. Yet still she continued to fall.

Flailing desperately and nearing unconsciousness, Kaiya's eyes spotted a tiny glint of light. It took on a familiar shape, but she could not put a name to it. Forcing herself to stay awake, she stared at the light as it came closer. It shone brighter but still eluded her. If only she could grasp it, perhaps she would be saved. Struggling to lift her arm, Kaiya found it far too heavy. Her arm had become a part of the rock, and it would not obey her command. She stared at the light as her eyes slid shut, her final sight that of its fading silver glow.

Bolting upright, Kaiya woke from her dream and stared into the fire. Looking up to the sky, she stared upon the same stars she had seen before falling asleep. The ground beneath her trembled, and she braced herself, fearing the opening of the chasm she had envisioned. Fortunately, no such event occurred. The trembling subsided, and all was quiet once more.

Disturbed by her dream, Kaiya hugged her knees to her chest. She stared into the darkness, wondering what it could mean. Perhaps it was simply a product of her lack of sleep, but it left her with a feeling that it was much more. A soft breeze caressed her cheek, reminding her of its presence. *It was a message,* she decided.

It was still an hour before dawn, but Kaiya couldn't wait. She extinguished the fire and took one last look at the stars before heading back down the hill. Her mind whirling, she marched toward home. Within an hour, she stood upon the hill beside her family's farm. The home where she had grown up quietly awaited her arrival, smoke already drifting from the chimney. Kaiya's own house stood a few hundred yards behind it, her refuge from the world. The small cottage had been lovingly built by her father nearly five years ago, after he decided she would never choose a husband.

With a soft sigh, Kaiya proceeded to her parents' home and peeked inside the door. Her mother, Kassie, busied herself in the kitchen despite the early hour. To Kaiya's surprise, her father, Darvil, sat in his favorite chair, a blanket over his lap. Though he had grown thin and pale over the past two years, Kaiya still wasn't used to him not being able to work. Normally, he would already be out in the fields, tending to the sheep. But the farm had proved too much for him in his failing health. Swallowing the sharp pain that came into her throat, Kaiya moved to her father's side.

"How are you feeling?" she asked.

"Never better," he replied, grinning.

She leaned in to hug him, noticing more white lines in his thick, red beard. "I love you, Papa," she whispered before letting go. It seemed she couldn't tell him those words enough lately.

Kassie appeared in the doorway, her gray hair pulled back into a neat bun. Holding a steaming bowl of porridge in her hands, she asked, "Are you hungry, dear?"

Kaiya shook her head and watched as her mother delivered the bowl to her father. "Careful, it's hot," she said at the same time as her mother.

Darvil rolled his eyes. "You two look alike, and now you sound alike," he said, a playful tone to his voice.

"What brings you here so early?" Kassie asked, taking a seat. She patted the cushion next to her, inviting her daughter to sit.

Kaiya remained standing. "There's trouble," she began. "I don't know what it is, but something is happening."

"Is it to do with the tremors?" Kassie asked.

Surprised by the response, Kaiya paused a moment. Her mother had always been intuitive, knowing what Kaiya was up to sometimes before she was aware herself. The two had always been close, but sometimes Kassie's perceptions were eerily correct. "Yes," Kaiya finally replied. "I also had a disturbing dream, a gift from the wind."

"Sounds like a gift worth returning," Darvil commented. "Why is it always your job to fix everything?"

"Because my sweet girl is special," Kassie answered, her eyes twinkling.

"If I didn't help when it was needed, I wouldn't be your daughter," Kaiya said. Her father was a kind-hearted man, always willing to lend a hand to the other farmers when they needed it. The lesson hadn't been lost on his only daughter. "I might have to go away for a few days," she continued. "I have to figure out what's going on." If her dream was correct, she might have to travel high into the mountains. "Will you take care of my dogs while I'm away?" she asked.

"Of course," her mother replied.

Leaning in, Kaiya kissed both her parents before heading out. In the fields, she spotted her two eldest brothers. They had arrived last year to tend the farm in their father's stead. Kaiya loved the farm, but she was no farmer. Her knowledge of agriculture was lacking, but she was able to shift the winds favorably to bring the rains as needed. It was the least she could do.

With a wave to her brothers, she proceeded to her own house. Greeting her were two dogs, one a black-and-tan herding dog named Doozle, and a smaller red-and-white dog named Flip. They greeted her with gusto, nearly knocking her to the ground to lick her face.

"Settle down, boys," she told them. "You behave for Mum while I'm away."

The dogs looked at her with all-too-knowing eyes. They missed her already.

"None of that," she said, stroking each on their backs and scratching at their ears. "I'll be back soon."

Grabbing a leather bag from her closet, she stuffed it with her warmest clothing and a blanket. Despite it being summertime here, higher elevations would still be bitterly cold. As she opened the door to leave, the dogs bolted into the field, greeting her brothers and prancing playfully. They were in good hands.

Kassie stood on the porch, waiting for her daughter to pass by. As Kaiya moved into sight, Kassie called, "Take this with you."

Kaiya retrieved the bundle containing a fresh loaf of bread and some dried fruit. "Thanks, Mum," she said. Her mother had always prided herself in her kitchen, and no child of hers ever went away hungry.

"You stay safe," her mother said, squeezing her close.

"I will," Kaiya promised. "You take care of Papa— and yourself too."

Glancing back only once, Kaiya pressed on along the rocky path that would lead her into town. It was the best place to start her investigation. News didn't reach the farmlands quickly, but the town was always full of chatter. Besides that, there was a friend she had neglected to visit.

Continuing along the path, she couldn't shake the feeling that someone was tracking her movements. She turned around and scanned the area but spotted no one. Still the feeling remained. It was different than the feeling of being watched. She couldn't quite describe it, but it was as if someone were aware of her movements, without being able to see or hear her. It could only be using magic, which troubled her further because she could not sense who or what it was. This was a force unknown. Whether it was friend or foe remained to be seen.

Chapter 3

Squinting her eyes at the afternoon sun, Tashi cursed its brazenness. How dare it rain down its light while Annin still lay abed, suffering convulsions and fever? What right did the world have to continue to turn when one so beautiful was dying? Tashi was no fool. She knew her sister would not last the day. Whatever she did, Annin would perish, and no god would intervene. How she hated them, both the good and the evil. What use were they to anyone?

Over the past few days, Tashi had gone from doubting all gods to begging for their assistance. She had finally come to this conclusion: Anything being worshipped as a god was a god, whether real or imagined. All that was certain was that she detested them all. They had refused to help her people, and that made the gods her enemy.

As High Priestess she was expected to tend to the spiritual needs of her tribe, but how could she continue to do so when she no longer had faith? If she spoke against the gods, her own tribe would exile her. That meant she would not be allowed to care for her sister's child. Tashi had no option but to play along, filling the role she was born to until the day she died. And then the burden would pass to her niece.

The child, who would not earn a name until she passed one year of age, would be forced into the same life as Tashi, never being free to choose any other path. *Perhaps the girl will truly be able to converse with the gods, assuming they listen to anyone,* Tashi mused. She had failed, but there was always a chance for the child, as long as she managed to survive. So far she had taken well to the goat's milk, readily suckling it from the tip of a ram's horn fashioned by the doula. The thought of her lovely niece brought a smile to the priestess's face. *I will not fail her as I have my sister.*

Nearing her sister's hut, Tashi paused outside the flap. At the edge of her vision, she spied a shadow, moving in the distance, but when she turned to face it, nothing was there. She stepped inside, observing first the doula, who cradled the cooing infant in her arms. Annin lay motionless upon her mattress, her face and hair dripping with sweat. Tashi's feet grew heavy as she approached her sister's form.

"Annin," she whispered, squeezing the girl's hand.

Annin stirred, her eyes barely opening, but a weak smile appeared on her lips. "My daughter," she struggled to say.

"She is beautiful and strong," Tashi replied.

Annin attempted to nod, but her head was far too heavy. Her heart yearned to hold her child, to nurse her at her breast and clutch her to her heart. Those days would never come. Her life was at an end, and she had made peace with that. "Sister," she whispered.

Tashi leaned closer to her sister. "I'm here," she said.

"You must care for her," Annin said, struggling for breath. "She…she…"

"I swear to you," Tashi stated. "She will survive, she will grow strong, and she will want for nothing in this life." She combed her fingers through her sister's hair and patted her cheek. Tears dripped from her eyes, splashing against the mattress. Her head felt heavy and thick, throbbing from back to front. *Be strong for her*, Tashi thought, squeezing her eyes shut. *For both of them.*

Annin fluttered her eyelids but did not speak. Her sister's words had not gone unheard. Despite her weakening body, she could rest peacefully knowing her child was safe. Resigning herself to her fate, she allowed her muscles to relax. She never spoke again.

Refusing to let go of her sister's hand, Tashi sat cross-legged on the dirt floor despite the pain in her heart. She wanted to run from the hut, screaming and raving. All in her path would flee in terror, or she would curse them as she had the gods. Her own people would fear her, ever believing the High Priestess had power over all their lives. But she could not leave the hut. There was nothing to do but sit, waiting for the end that was soon to come.

Wracked with fever, Annin's body faded quickly. Each breath came at great effort, her heart failing. Tashi could do nothing but watch. As the sun disappeared from the sky, Annin sighed softly to the evening's first star, her soul released to the night. Tashi laid her head against her sister's chest and sobbed, too grief-stricken to utter a sound. Her sister and dearest friend was gone forever.

"Tashi, you must tend her soul," the doula whispered softly, still clutching the baby to her breast. "She must find her way to the life that follows."

Tashi shot up from the ground, a fire in her eyes. "I know my duty," she spat. Without another word, the priestess pulled her sister's arms, forcing the girl into a sitting position. Bending Annin's knees, she pushed them against the girl's chest. Positioning the girl's arms around her knees, she whispered a prayer for the dead. Her sister had been ever faithful to the gods, and Tashi would honor her as such.

Wrapping the woolen blanket around her sister's body, Tashi pulled it taut. Annin's body would sit in prayer posture throughout the ceremony to come. Stepping outside the hut, Tashi looked upon the faces of her tribe. Many had gathered outside the young mother's hut, offering their support to one in need.

"Annin's soul has departed," Tashi announced. "Who will carry her to the pyre?"

Three large men stepped forward, one of them Annin's mate. Their heads held low, they spoke no words as they entered the hut and gently lifted the young woman's body. Tashi led the procession, followed by her sister's shell. The rest of the villagers followed single file, bearing torches to light the darkness.

High on a hill stood a mound of stones, the only permanent structure made by these nomadic people. Annin's body was set upon it, and the men backed away in silence. Despite her growing dizziness, Tashi began the death chant, beginning with a single mournful cry to the darkness. Two women joined at her side, bearing the wooden masks of death. Together, the trio donned the masks, representing the three judges one meets in the life to come. One face of sorrow, one of anger, and one of joy. They danced among the villagers, crying to the night, their voices shrieking.

For nearly an hour, the dance continued, all the while Tashi's head continued throbbing. Her neck was stiff, her skin too hot. The dance could not end soon enough. The dancers dropped to the ground, landing on their knees and lowering their heads. The villagers followed suit, kneeling before the mound.

Removing her mask, Tashi stood and offered one final prayer to the gods. Her voice cracked as she uttered the words, her heart believing none of them. There would be no beauty waiting for Tashi in death, but perhaps there was for her faithful sister. Finishing the prayer, she approached the mound and laid a hand gently on her sister's head. "Goodbye, sweet sister," she whispered. Tossing a handful of powder over the blanket, she stepped away and looked up at the stars.

The villagers walked forward, each with a torch in hand. Offering the flames to the bundled woman, they freed her from her worldly restraint. No longer would the shell inhibit her spirit. She would rise again in a better world.

Tashi stumbled through the darkness, not bothering to carry a torch of her own. She had to get away. There was no more to be done for Annin. Sobbing, she blindly found her way back to her hut and collapsed onto her own mattress. Burying her face in her pillow, she fell into a fitful sleep.

Nightmares of monsters, their dark forms dancing, invaded Tashi's mind. They moved closer and closer, approaching the flaming remains of the young mother, but Tashi did not fear them. "You will not take her soul!" she shouted. To take her sister, they would have to get through her first. She would fight them with her bare hands if she had to. The shadows closed in on Tashi, forcing her to the ground, but she refused to cry out. "Take me," she hissed, "but you will never take her!"

Tashi woke before sunrise, the pain behind her eyes proof enough that she had barely slept. A shadow moved across the central fire of her hut, but it disappeared before she could identify it. The fire sizzled, but no vision appeared.

"Stay away, Mother," Tashi said to the flames. She would not have her mother blaming her for Annin's death. "I did all I could," she whispered.

Another shadow moved outside the flap, and Tashi rushed forward to catch it. Instead of a monster, she found the huddled form of Koli, who had been Annin's mate.

"Priestess," Koli said. "What will you do to safeguard the life of Annin's child? My child."

What could Tashi do? She couldn't save her sister, so how did she plan to save her niece? "I don't know," she admitted. "The gods…" she started to say, but found no fitting words to finish the thought.

"There must be a sacrifice," he said. "Without it, the gods will do nothing."

For centuries the Ulihi tribe had offered blood sacrifices to the gods in exchange for blessings. There were tales of great successes in battle as well as the ending of droughts thanks to the sacrifices made by the tribe. However, there had been many sacrifices to save the children these past ten years, but nothing had removed the curse from the tribe. No child had survived, and the sacrifices had been wasted. The gods refused to act.

"My sister has already been sacrificed," Tashi said. Her eyes stung from the tears that could no longer run, and she rubbed her fists against the dryness.

"We must be ready by daybreak," Koli insisted. "It will be done."

Tashi swallowed hard and stared at the man before her. He was large, a warrior among her people. He stood bare-chested and proud, determination in his dark eyes. Numerous strands of beads hung around his neck, and a row of precisely carved scars adorned his ribs. He would have fought many battles were there battles to be fought. Instead, his marks symbolized the hunt, and the animals he had bested to feed his tribe. He was not a man to be argued with.

"I am High Priestess," Tashi said, stepping forward. "No man or woman commands me."

"The gods command you," Koli shot back, "and they demand a sacrifice."

"And they have had it," she replied, finding more tears than she believed she possessed.

Koli shook his head. "It is not enough," he said, his manner softening. "Please, Tashi. For the child to be named, there must be a sacrifice."

"The gods have not found their way to our people in many years," Tashi said. "What makes you think this time will be different?"

"Because it has to be," he said.

Tashi stared into his eyes and saw his certainty. Too many still believed in the gods, too many still so foolish. "I will assemble the villagers," she finally said.

Koli grabbed her wrist as she began to walk away. "The death of the infants these many years were not your doing," he said. "You were not High Priestess when this began. Your mother was."

Looking him up and down, Tashi said, "My mother was a faithful priestess." How could he dare blame her mother for such tragedy?

"She drove the gods away," Koli went on. "You must bring them back."

Jerking her arm away from him, Tashi crossed the center of the village and stared at the horizon. Koli could not possibly know. He was older than her, but he knew nothing of the lot of a priestess. Tashi's mother had revealed to her the truth behind her profession. It was merely the crafting of potions and singing of chants. The rest fell to the villagers to believe or not. The gods had nothing to do with it. One either chose to believe or didn't. It mattered not. Tashi's mother had chosen to believe, as had her sister. The deaths of so many infants had another cause, one unknown to the priestesses and doulas.

Koli proceeded to gather the villagers as Tashi continued looking toward the sunrise. Seeing them all assembled, she shook her head. *A sacrifice will not fix our problems,* she thought. *We need true magic, not this shameful display.*

Standing before her people, she announced, "Koli insists on a sacrifice to protect the life of his child. Is anyone willing?"

43

One old woman stood, propping herself on a wooden stick. "I will go to the gods in the child's place," the woman said proudly.

"No," Koli said. "You are old and near death anyway. Such a sacrifice means nothing to the gods."

The old woman bowed her head and took a seat, not willing to argue with the warrior.

"I will go," Koli continued. "The gods can have me."

The life of a strong man had always carried more weight with the gods, at least in centuries past. Only the most pressing matters were handled in such a way. It was preferable to sacrifice enemy tribesmen who had been captured in battle, but Tashi's was the only tribe left. It had to be one of her own.

"Very well," she said. Pulling a thin dagger from the holster on her arm, she held it up to the first rays of the sun. Its golden hue reflected in the metal as Koli knelt before her and tilted his head backward. Shouting to the gods, Tashi implored them to take the life of this man and look favorably upon the life of the infant. The villagers trilled in time with the priestess's chant, granting their approval of the exchange.

All fell silent as Tashi plunged the blade into Koli's neck, the red life force spurting back at her, coating her arms and legs. She turned her head away, feeling the eyes of the gods upon her. They were laughing, mocking the futile effort. Koli had died for no reason. The gods would not assist her. She had no use for them, and they had no favors for her.

Preparing Koli's body as she had her sister's, Tashi cursed the waste of life. Koli had loved her sister and wanted to follow her in death. *That is why he volunteered,* she told herself. Remembering the look in his eyes as he insisted on the sacrifice gave her pause. He truly believed this would save his child. Would it have saved Annin? Tashi would never know. It was too late to trade her own life. There was no sacrifice that could bring Annin back to the living.

Chapter 4

Kaiya arrived in the town, the constant ringing of hammers upon anvils echoing in her ears. It was rarely quiet in dwarven towns during the daytime. As she approached the smithy, the ground rumbled beneath her, and she reached for her magic to keep herself upright. Metal implements clanged and rattled, the blacksmith himself rolling out of the way to avoid falling objects. It lasted only a few seconds, but it was enough to ruffle the man's temper.

Staring up at Kaiya from his position on the ground, he asked, "Can't you put a stop to this damn shaking?"

"Not yet," she replied, honestly, but with a note of pride in her voice. She was no earth mage, but if she could find a way to quiet the mountain, she would do it.

Passing the smith, she headed for the rune carver's stall located directly behind the smithy. A tall elf with dark waist-length hair greeted her with a friendly smile. His brown eyes sparkled with a hint of mischief, but before he could open his mouth to speak, Trin shoved him from behind.

"You're in my way, elf," the rune carver said. Shaking his head, he added, "Always standing about."

"Maybe you should give him more work to do," Kaiya jibed. Galen had apprenticed for Trin for six years, and he'd learned nearly all there was to know about dwarven runes. There wasn't much else for the elf to do in the small town, but Kaiya knew why he stayed. He hoped to remain close to her.

A few years back, the two had been romantically involved. Kaiya, however, wasn't ready to settle into a relationship. As a sorceress, her life would extend for many centuries. There was plenty of time to find a partner, if indeed she wanted one. The only thing tying her to this place was her parents. She loved them dearly, but they would not live forever. When they no longer had need of her, she intended to travel with the wind as her only companion.

Not that Galen made a bad traveling companion, and he would likely travel anywhere at her request. But he was content to stay in one place as long as there were books to read. He spent most of his daylight hours assisting Trin, but his evenings were spent in intense study, including the history of the dwarves, their ancient language, and the geology of the mountain itself. It made for interesting conversations, and the two remained close friends. A true loner, Kaiya doubted anything more would ever come of their relationship.

"He already has me do the majority of his work," Galen replied with a smile. "Trin spends most of his time whittling stone animals for his grandchildren."

Trin glared at the elf, his silver beard quivering slightly. "One time I did that," he replied. "One time." He held up a single finger as near to Galen's face as he could reach.

After a moment staring at each other, both men laughed. Such was their friendship, plenty of joking to pass the tedious hours of work their chosen profession required.

When he'd finished laughing, Galen turned his attention back to Kaiya. "Someone was looking for you this morning," he told her.

"Who?" she asked. "Did you send him to the farm?"

"It was someone from one of the mines up north, and I didn't catch his name," the elf replied. "He headed off for a drink without saying anything else."

Kaiya shook her head. It was just like a dwarf man to start drinking before breakfast. No wonder she had considered an elf for a partner before any dwarf. "You have no idea what he wanted?"

"All I know was he was looking for a sorceress, and that could only mean you," Galen replied, reaching for a smooth black stone. He placed it on the counter with a loud thud, earning him a cutting glance from Trin. "I'll help you find him if you like," he offered.

"You have work to do," Kaiya replied. "We'll talk later." She was interested in getting Galen's take on her vision and the tremors, but it was more urgent to speak to the visitor. It was no coincidence he had shown up this morning.

Hurrying along the dirt roads, Kaiya ignored everyone in her path. The merchants hawked their wares as she strode past, but she wasn't listening. Her sights set on the tavern, she pressed on to the farthest edge of town near the mines.

Despite the early hour, the tavern buzzed with activity. A miner grinned drunkenly at the sorceress as he exited, holding the door open for the lady. Bobbing her head in thanks, she stepped inside, her nose tingling from the strong scent of hops and pipe smoke.

Several men sat inside, and one large woman stood behind the bar, casually conversing with a customer. Only one man was unfamiliar, so he had to be the one looking for her. Visitors were few in this town. Kaiya went straight to his table and pulled up a chair. The man eyed her a moment, wiping the foam away from his curly, brown beard.

"You the sorceress?" he asked.

Kaiya gave a single nod. "I am, and I heard you were looking for me."

The dwarf took a long sip from his frothy mug before banging it on the table. He let out a long belch before speaking. "Name's Raad," he began. "There's trouble up north, and the foreman decided you were the woman to deal with it."

"What kind of trouble?" she asked impatiently.

"It started as tremors," Raad explained. "Just enough to unnerve us at first, but then it got worse. Soon the ground was shaking us so bad, you'd think we were all staggering drunk." He tapped his empty mug on the table, signaling the bartender for a refill. Once he had it in hand, he continued. "Damn avalanche caused a cave-in and injured thirteen workers. It took days to dig them out."

Kaiya sighed. "If the tremors kept happening, why would you go inside the mine?" She asked despite knowing the answer. Dwarves could be quite greedy, and iron ore wasn't the only mineral found in the northernmost mines. The rarest of all gemstones, painite—better known as Dwarf's Heart—was also found in small quantities. Kings of all lands craved these gems, which could be refined only by the finest elven craftsmen.

"There's work to be done, miss," Raad replied. "We don't travel that far north to sit around, tremors or not."

"Surely you've experienced avalanches before," Kaiya said. "What brought you to find me?"

"It wasn't just one avalanche; it was three," Raad said, wiping his mouth with his sleeve. "We've got miners out with injuries, and it's slowing down production. Foreman thought you might be able to put a stop to it."

"It sounds like you need an earth mage, not me," she replied.

"You know as well as I do that there aren't any around these parts," Raad said. "I'd never heard of a wizard that wasn't an elf, and they don't come here. We take the gems to them, but they're not interested in visiting us."

Kaiya knew well that the elves of the isles weren't readily available to lend their assistance to the dwarves. The two races barely tolerated each other, the dwarves despising the elves for their arrogance, and the elves despising the dwarves for their boorish nature. It was a rare thing to see the two getting along.

"You're the only wizard around here who might be of use to us," Raad said. "We could sure use your help."

Contemplating a moment, Kaiya felt uneasy. Suspicions of a presence within the mountain had not left her, the images from her vision still playing in her head. "I'll come with you," she stated. "I'll do whatever I can to help."

"Much obliged," Raad said, finishing his ale. Extending his arm, he shook the sorceress's hand.

At the miner's touch, Kaiya felt a sudden surge of fear. There was something more that he wasn't telling her. "Is there something else I need to know?" she asked.

Raad shook his head. "Foreman Daro will explain everything when we get there." He looked away quickly.

Kaiya did not press the matter. Whatever he was hiding would not change her decision. She had agreed to go, and she would keep her word regardless of the possible danger. Her vision was leading her higher into the mountains, whether she traveled with Raad or alone. "When do you plan to leave?" she asked.

"I'd like another drink, and then I'm all yours," he said, flashing a smile.

"I'll meet you near the forges on the north side of town," she said. "We can set out from there."

Raad nodded his agreement and headed over to the bar, empty mug in hand. Kaiya pushed her way through a group of miners who were blocking her way to the exit. No magic was needed. They were too drunk to put up a struggle as the determined woman elbowed past them.

Not two steps outside the tavern, Kaiya stopped short, surprised by the sight in front of her. Galen waved cheerfully as he jogged to meet her.

"I thought you had work to do," Kaiya said, her hands moving to her hips.

Galen waved the comment away. "I wanted to make sure you found your visitor," he said, grinning.

"I did," she replied, starting to walk.

Galen kept pace at her side. "So what did he want?"

"There's trouble at the mines," she said.

"Naturally," the elf commented. "What kind of trouble?"

Kaiya paused her walking. "The kind that doesn't concern you," she said. "Why are you so nosey all of a sudden?" It wasn't like him to ply her with questions. He was typically laid-back and willing to let her have her secrets. She was, after all, a sorceress.

"I know something's troubling you," he said sincerely. "Those tremors are a warning."

"What makes you say that?" she wondered. Did the elf know something she didn't?

"I've done a lot of reading in my lifetime," he began. "And I've lived a long time in the Vale beneath these mountains. There have never been earthquakes in my lifetime."

"That doesn't mean they couldn't be natural," she said, willing her voice to stay steady. What good would it do to worry her friend with her own suspicions?

"You're hiding something," Galen said. "Whatever it is, I want to help."

"I don't even know if I need help yet," she replied. "Until I've gone to the mines to see for myself, I won't know what's going on."

"So you do plan to leave," he said. "I figured that miner came to fetch you for something."

"Yes, he did," she said. "The Dwarf's Heart mines have become dangerous, and people have been hurt. It could be natural, it could be something else. That's what I'm going to figure out."

"I'll go with you," Galen said, his tone resolute.

"I appreciate the offer, but it's not going to be a fun trip," she replied. Galen made a good companion for travel, but this wasn't a vacation. This was serious business, and he would try to make light of it. She feared he would only prove a distraction from her investigation. "It could also be dangerous," she added.

"Then you might need me to rescue you," he said, chuckling. "Plus it'll give me a chance to work with Dwarf's Heart. Trin will be jealous."

Kaiya pursed her lips and stared at the elf.

"I'm going whether you like it or not, so please say you'll like it," he said.

Kaiya sighed and glanced up at his warm, brown eyes. Though he had few skills in mountain survival, and his magical skills were even fewer, he could offer something far more valuable. His friendship would be a bit of light in a dark place. The wind rustled his hair, the ends tickling against Kaiya's cheek. In that touch, she felt a sense of family. Here was a man willing to walk to the ends of the earth with her, wanting nothing but her friendship in return. "I'd be grateful for your company," she heard herself say.

* * * * *

Half an hour passed and then an hour, Galen all the while leaning against the edge of a stone well. Kaiya clenched her teeth and stared down the dirt road, impatiently awaiting the appearance of Raad.

"Relax," Galen said. "He'll be along soon."

Kaiya was anxious to get going. "He said *one* more drink," she grunted, still staring at the path. After two more minutes, Kaiya threw her hands in the air. "That's it. I'm going to fetch him." She started off but stopped, seeing the brown-bearded dwarf staggering toward her.

Galen chuckled. "Looks like he had one more dozen."

Kaiya fumed but managed to hold her tongue. Her only regret was not leaving without him. She could use magic to find the mine's location. Raad's company was not needed.

He hiccupped and nodded as he presented himself before his traveling companions. His eyes stopped on Galen, the dwarf tilting his head sideways for a better look at the elf who stood three feet taller than himself. "You a real elf?" he asked.

Galen didn't bother to contain his laughter. "Something like that," he replied.

"Well, I'll be the son of a stone eater," Raad said, still staring at Galen. The elf wore dwarven-style clothes, crafted from wool and accented with dwarven runic symbols. "You could pass for an extra-tall dwarf. I've never seen one of your kind not wearing those fancy robes that hide all your magic spells underneath."

"Galen isn't one of the Enlightened Elves you've dealt with," Kaiya explained, her tone annoyed. "He's a Westerling Elf, and he lives here in this village." She glanced over at the elf. "He might as well be one of us, so if you've got a problem with him you can just sit on it."

This time Raad and Galen both laughed.

"I meant no offense, sorceress," Raad said, his cheeks rosy from too much drink. "He's a rare sight is all I meant."

Galen shook his head, clearly amused by Kaiya's response to the miner.

Sighing, Kaiya said, "You can call me Kaiya, not sorceress. Do you think you're drunk enough to find your way back to the mine?" Many dwarf men insisted they could navigate better after they'd had a few.

"I could use a few more to tell you the truth," Raad said with a grin. "But it's time to go, so we go. Too bad there isn't fine ale up at the mining camp like you have here."

"There's no ale?" Galen asked, wrinkling his brow. "I'd think the miners would go on strike."

"Oh there's ale, all right," Raad said. "But it doesn't ferment properly in the cold up there."

"Why not just import it?" the elf asked.

"Too expensive," Raad replied.

"You're mining the rarest mineral in all Nōl'Deron," Galen said. "Cost shouldn't be an issue."

Raad shrugged. "It's not like we miners get much benefit from that. Those stones are rare finds among the iron."

Kaiya swiveled her head to look at the miner. "They don't share the profits with the workers?"

"We get a small bonus," Raad replied. "But the mineral isn't worth nearly as much in its raw form. It's the shapers and polishers who make out like bandits."

"That doesn't seem fair," Kaiya replied. "The miners do the dangerous part. You should charge the elves more."

Raad laughed. "You want us to argue with wizards?" He slapped his hand against his leg. "Maybe you can negotiate that for us."

"Maybe I will," she replied. With determination in her step, she strode on, leading the way along the northern path. The wizards of the isles did not frighten her. They were certainly powerful, but the wind was on her side. She came by her powers naturally. The Enlightened Elves tortured themselves through countless hours of magical training, all in an effort to prove their superiority over each other. Their methods were flawed in her eyes, and she did not consider them a threat.

As she looked into the distance, the memory of the presence climbed back into her thoughts. Or was she sensing it again? Something was definitely out there, and its mind was growing stronger, though it still hid itself somewhere among the mountains. The hairs on the back of her neck stood up, a slight discomfort coming over her stomach. All was not well.

Chapter 5

It was just past midday when the trio finally set out, and the summer sun offered up its warmth as they journeyed along the dirt path. Fields of green lay to either side, but only steps ahead, the grass became sparse, unable to take root in the rocky mountain soil. Soon the travelers would be immersed in stone, the smooth path carved by the dwarves their only scenery.

"How is the weather up north?" Galen asked, attempting to fill the silence.

"Cold," Raad grunted. He leaned forward slightly as he walked, the weight of his backpack heavy.

Squinting his eyes slightly, Galen asked, "What have you go in there?"

"Cask," the dwarf replied, his white teeth shining.

"Will you be sharing?" the elf asked.

Raad shook his head. "You can get this stuff any time. I might not be back this way for years."

"Well, save it until we've arrived," Kaiya said, scanning the surroundings. "We need to keep our minds sharp." With every step, her worry grew. She tried to tell herself she was only being paranoid, but still she couldn't shake the feeling that something was out there—waiting, watching, and planning its first, or possibly next, move.

"What's wrong, Kaiya?" Galen asked, his tone sincere.

"I wish I knew," she responded. "Maybe Raad could shed more light on the situation."

The dwarf seemed confused. "How so?" he asked.

"There's more than what you've told me," she said. "Why don't you let me in on the rest of the story?"

"The tremors started weeks ago," the miner began, "but we ignored it mostly. That sort of thing happens from time to time, but there's nothing to be done about it. We went on with our work, but the shaking kept getting worse." He shrugged, wondering what else the sorceress wanted to know.

"And then?" she asked, her eyes focused ahead. The light was fading quickly as they climbed higher in the mountains, and she hoped to know the full story by nightfall. Perhaps then her dreams would reveal something significant.

"The rest is best left to Foreman Daro," Raad said. "I couldn't explain it if I wanted to."

"Try," Kaiya insisted.

"There are strange things in the highest reaches of the world," Galen broke in. "Perhaps you encountered one of them." He smiled slightly at the miner.

"Maybe," Raad muttered. To Kaiya, he said, "You're the sorceress, so figuring these things out is your job, not mine. I was sent to fetch you, and I have. There's nothing more to say."

Kaiya said nothing but focused her magic to the dwarf behind her. His mind was a jumble, likely due to the alcohol he had been drinking. Strange images came to the surface, but all she could make out were rocks. No matter how deep she pried, only rocks came into view. *Miners,* she thought, disappointed. Her skill of probing another's mind clearly needed a lot more work.

65

The path narrowed until the trio was forced into close quarters, walls of gray rock on either side of them. It gave Galen a claustrophobic feeling, but he did his best to hide it. The dwarves were far more at home in small spaces than the elf. He found himself holding his breath for long intervals, his discomfort written on his face.

"We'll be through this in a few minutes," Kaiya quietly reassured him. Though she was not yet able to fully probe the elf's complex mind, she could read his body language quite well.

To Galen's relief, the trio emerged unscathed only a hundred yards from where they had entered. Gone were the green grasses of the previous landscape, replaced by black rocks and dirt with only sparse patches of greenery. The sun had nearly disappeared from view, its pink rays barely able to reach so high in the mountains at this hour.

"We might as well make camp," Raad said. "It'll be dark in a few minutes." Without waiting for the others to concur, he removed his backpack and tossed it to the ground. "Nights are cold up here, but I expect a sorceress can fix that," he said with a grin.

Kaiya nodded. Arranging some loose rocks into a neat pile, she projected silver sparks at their center. A white flame glowed to life, providing far more warmth than a fire of such a small size should have been able to produce.

Raad nodded approvingly. "That's a handy trick," he commented. Looking to Galen, he asked, "Don't all elves do magic?"

"To some extent," Galen replied, taking a seat near the fire. "I'm not much of a wizard myself."

Filling a mug with the ale from his cask, the dwarf asked, "What do you do, Elf?"

"You can call me Galen," the elf replied. "And I'm apprentice to a rune carver."

"Overpriced baubles," Raad grumbled before pressing the mug to his lips.

"The price reflects the quality," Galen explained, unfazed by the dwarf's words. "A master rune carver spends countless hours on each creation, imbuing the item with its power."

"I've never had that kind of money to spare," Raad said.

Rolling her eyes, Kaiya cut in, "You might if you didn't spend all your coin on drink."

Raad scrunched his face, hurt by the accusation. "This cask is a rare find! It's finer than any you'll find up north, and alcohol is guaranteed to work its magic better than enchanted swords and axes."

"That's not all rune carving is," Galen explained. "Yes, there are weapons, but there are practical items as well. Take mining picks for example. One inlaid with runes would carve rock faster and with less effort than what you're used to."

Shrugging, the miner replied, "I've never worked with one like that, but Foreman Daro would probably agree with you. He wears a runed trinket on a string around his neck. Says it brings him luck." He paused to take a swig out of his mug before asking, "You think it actually works?"

Galen shook his head. "It's impossible to say without examining it. Most runed items have a specific purpose, so 'luck' wouldn't necessarily be its intention. Perhaps it makes the Dwarf's Heart easier to detect."

"He'd be richer if it did," Raad said, chuckling. "Daro's a strange one. He likes to spend good money on charms and magic items. He claims to have quite a collection at home. I suppose all that believing in spells and enchantments is why he sent me to fetch a sorceress."

Rosy cheeked, Raad checked the stopper in his cask to be sure it was secured. Glancing at Kaiya, he joked, "Wouldn't want to lose any." Rolling his backpack into a makeshift pillow, he lay back with his feet nearest the fire.

With an amused smirk, Kaiya realized that Raad had consumed only one mug of ale. Apparently he was capable of controlling himself, if only to save the drink for a more jovial occasion.

Galen scooted closer to Kaiya. "Are you cold?" he asked.

"Not at all," she replied honestly.

"Me neither," he said, looking toward the fire.

A silence passed between them, neither of them sure what to say. Kaiya rested her hands on her knees and turned her gaze to the stars. Galen decided it was best to give her some space, and moved away before stretching himself out on the ground. The rocks made for an uncomfortable bed, prompting him to toss and turn for several minutes.

Unable to contain her laughter, Kaiya said, "Raad's fast asleep already, but you look like you're on a bed of nails."

Galen smiled and sat up. "It's not exactly a feather bed," he replied. "I'd give anything for a soft patch of grass."

"Like you had in the Vale," Kaiya said. The Vale below the mountains was home to the most beautiful forests Kaiya had ever seen. The silver trees grew large enough to live inside, and a crystal blue river flowed along its edge. It was a place of magic and safety, its constant springtime climate giving vitality to all manner of plants and creatures. It was a far cry from the mountains. "Don't you miss your home?" she asked.

"Of course," he replied, "but there is much I can learn here in the mountains." He flashed a smile, "And you can't beat the company."

Kaiya hated herself for blushing. Galen still had feelings for her, and she couldn't deny that she cared a great deal for him. But both had centuries ahead of them. There was no need to rush a relationship. This was a sentiment she reminded herself of again and again but occasionally had a hard time believing. His dark eyes glistening in the firelight warmed Kaiya's heart. "I'm glad you came along," she said.

"Me too," he replied.

A symphony of crickets began a new overture as the stars burned brightly in the darkened sky. The pair shared no more words, each eventually drifting off to sleep, dreaming of lands far more inviting than the barren mountainside.

*****

Kaiya woke before the others, finding herself still in a seated position. Years of practice at meditation had left her able to rest without sprawling herself on the ground and leaving herself vulnerable. On this journey, she was grateful for the skill. The presence she had sensed was once again manifesting itself at the edge of her mind. The wind grew still, her ears straining to hear its words.

"Morning," a voice mumbled.

Kaiya startled at the sound and looked over at Raad, surprised to see him awake. "You're up early," she commented.

Running thick fingers through coarse hair, he replied, "I've been on the early shift since I was old enough to swing a pick. I couldn't sleep through a sunrise if I wanted to."

The sorceress glanced at Galen, who slept soundly near the fire. Apparently he had found a way to move beyond his discomfort. She smiled as she watched him, happy to have his companionship. Whatever might lie in store for their future, Kaiya knew he would remain a dear friend to the end.

Rising from her cross-legged position, she stretched her stiff muscles. By afternoon they should reach the mines, but it was going to be a tough day of walking over uneven terrain. Moving to Galen's side, she gently placed a hand on his arm and shook it.

The elf awoke groggy, rubbing the sleep from his eyes. Giving Kaiya a crooked smile, he attempted to smooth his hair into a presentable fashion.

"We should get moving," she said. "Unless, of course, you want to spend another night on the rocks."

Rubbing his lower back, he said, "It's not at the top of my list." His bones were used to softer beds, but he wouldn't dwell on the negative. Though his body was already aching, and the day's climb was sure to add to his discomfort, he was happy to travel beside his friend.

With a wave of her hand, Kaiya extinguished the fire and waited for her companions to gather their belongings. Slinging her own bag across her back, she waved for them to follow.

The travelers forged ahead, the landscape altering itself as they ascended along the path. What was once gray rock gave way to a light layer of snow, the winds shifting to bring the mountaintop's frigid air upon them.

With a laugh, Raad said, "Don't worry, it'll get worse." This was only the beginning of the weather he was used to. The mines lay in the higher reaches, in the shadow of the mountain's summit.

They pressed on, the weather becoming fierce. Snow swirled about them, forcing them to shield their eyes. After stumbling over a few large stones, Kaiya focused her mind to the wind. Though she lacked the ability to stop the snowstorm, she could make travel more tolerable. Holding her palm outward, she shifted the winds before her, cutting a narrow clearing through the air. This would allow her and her companions to see where they were going, and hopefully avoid some of the obstacles that were quickly being buried by the snowfall.

For more than two hours, heavy snowfall bombarded the freezing travelers. Their feet disappeared beneath them, buried in a blanket of white. Kaiya continued to hold her spell, slicing through the madness as they pressed onward. Finally, the snow relented to a softer, more tolerable level. Flakes of white still tumbled from the skies, but there was no longer a need for magic.

It would be another hour before the skies cleared, the snow retreating to the higher elevations. Raad's stomach gurgled loud enough for the others to hear, and he insisted on having a few bites to eat while the weather permitted.

"Just eat fast," Kaiya insisted, removing her pack. Reaching inside, she retrieved the meal her mother had prepared for her and shared it with her companions.

They nibbled hungrily, each of them eager to get moving again. The mines were growing nearer, and they might reach them before the next round of snow hit.

Raad poured himself a mug of ale and downed it in one long gulp. His cheeks becoming rosy, he said, "Gotta keep warm out here!"

"Let's get a move on," was Kaiya's only reply. She took one step forward and paused, struck by the sensation that they were not alone. Her mind raced, searching for the presence she had sensed before, but this was something different. She detected no magic, nor did she detect the presence of any sort of beast. This was a person, possibly more than one.

"What is it?" Galen asked, noticing her tensed posture.

Kaiya held a hand up to silence him as she swiveled her head to locate whoever was near. Movement caught her eye from high above, a glistening object descending from the sky. "Move!" she cried to the others as she spun to one side.

The shining tip of a spear landed in their midst, embedding itself in the frozen ground. The trio looked at one another, realizing they were under attack. A second spear followed the first, but Kaiya was ready. Steadying her hand, she forced the spear away, guiding it to rest at Raad's feet. He swooped to grab it, clutching the weapon in his hand.

When the third spear neared her location, Kaiya had had enough. She summoned a gust of wind, turning the spear and forcing it back toward its owner. A cry of surprise echoed through the mountains as the spear found its mark, nearly missing the man who had thrown it. It was not Kaiya's intention to hit him, but rather to let him know that she would not tolerate a continued attack.

The trio moved close together, staring ahead as their attackers moved into view. A group of no less than a dozen figures moved their way, led by a female figure in a long wooden mask. The mask's expression displayed anger, but the figure's body language displayed caution. With her head shaved smooth and rows of beads dangling across her chest, Kaiya knew the woman must be of some importance to these primitive people.

Kaiya furrowed her brow impatiently. "Why have you attacked us?" she demanded, shouting.

The masked woman moved closer, her ebony skin contrasting against the snow. In her hand she clutched a staff, the bleached white skull of a goat upon its end. "You have invaded our land!" the woman called back.

"You will come with us, and we will determine your fate!"

Raad laughed low in his throat. "I guess they don't know who they're dealing with," he said, nudging Kaiya slightly.

Raising her hands defensively, Kaiya prepared to defend herself and her companions. But the wind rustled her hair, whispering a message in her ear. To her surprise, she replied, "We will go with you."

Chapter 6

"Are you crazy?" Raad asked. "Those are mountain wild men!"

Her expression serene, Kaiya replied, "I know what I'm doing."

"I don't think you do," Raad stated, gripping the spear tighter. "You should blast these savages before they kill all three of us. They practice evil magic."

"What do you mean?" she asked.

"They've put curses on us miners before," he said. "Boils and dysentery are their favorite weapons besides the spear. They hate us. They don't want us in these mountains, and they'll kill any dwarf they can get their hands on."

"These people have no magic," Kaiya replied. "You're mistaken, and I won't harm them."

"Did you miss the part where they attacked us?" he asked, lifting the spear to her face.

"I miss nothing," she said, placing her hand on the spear shaft and lowering it. "Put this down before they think you're threatening them."

Raad stared open-mouthed at the sorceress. Taking a look at Galen, the dwarf weighed his options. "You agree with her, Elf?"

"I trust her judgment," Galen stated. "She won't let them harm us." His voice betrayed no hint of deception. If Kaiya did not fear these people, Galen would not.

With a huff, Raad tossed the spear to the ground in front of him. The attackers approached with caution, the masked figure leading the way.

Kaiya spread her arms in a nonthreatening manner. "We aren't here to hurt you," she said. "We will go with you to discuss our presence in your land. We want no trouble, only to pass through. Our kinsmen are in need of our help."

Removing her mask, Tashi studied the travelers before her. Raad was uninteresting. She had seen hundreds of miners before. But Kaiya's presence demanded a second look. Studying her face closely, she asked, "Are you a being of magic?"

"I am," Kaiya replied.

Tashi's eyes widened. She didn't know how, but she could sense the magic in this woman. It radiated from her, her power unmistakable. Never before had Tashi encountered a being of true magic, and it was both frightening and intriguing.

The warriors moved to a position behind the intruders and lowered their spears. The priestess led the way, heading back toward her tribe's village. Instead of continuing north, the travelers were forced in a westerly direction, rounding a steep hillside and hopping over a deep crag.

They descended slightly, taking the trio farther away from their original destination. The landscape smoothed, and a tiny village came into view. Evergreens surrounded it, stretching on to eternity, lifting their snow-covered boughs in praise of the life-giving sun. In the most beautiful stretch of the inhospitable mountains, the tribe had carved a home.

"Wait in there," Tashi commanded, pointing to a hut.

The three did not argue, instead stepping inside without a word. They sat cross-legged, facing the door flap and awaiting whatever might come through it.

"You've encountered these wild men before?" Kaiya asked Raad.

"I've seen them from a distance," he replied. "Mostly it's stories. Lots of miners have seen things, and some of our caravans have been attacked."

Galen shook his head. "These are the Ulihi. They keep mostly to themselves."

"How do you know?" Kaiya asked.

"I've read about them," the elf replied. "There are several old volumes that mention this tribe. Once they populated the entire mountain range and lived peacefully with the earliest dwarves. Now they've all but disappeared. I'm actually surprised these people are still living here."

"How do you know that's who we're dealing with?" Raad asked, his tone skeptical. These were undoubtedly the people the miners had encountered before, and they were anything but peaceful.

"Their clothing or lack thereof is a dead giveaway," Galen explained. "They have ebony skin, blessed by the hand of the mountain itself. It's said they're impervious to the cold."

"That would explain why they're scantily dressed," Kaiya replied. The tribesmen wore little more than colorful beaded collars, loin cloths, and goat-hair adornments on their ankles. The priestess wore only a bit more. By comparison, the dwarves wrapped themselves in thick woolen tunics and cloaks before traveling high in the mountains, and their faces still became raw and red from exposure. The Ulihi appeared not to notice the frigid temperatures, and they had managed to track Kaiya's group through heavy snowfall. She could understand why the miners thought these people practiced magic. In reality, they were doing what their ancestors had done for centuries, with no help from magic at all.

"There's also a theory that these are the ancestors of the dwarves," Galen added.

"You're speaking like there aren't two dwarves sitting next to you," Raad grumbled.

"Sorry," the elf replied. "What I should have said was, these people could likely be relatives of yours. It's speculated that some Ulihi refused to modernize when the rest of the dwarves moved lower in the mountains and built a new civilization. The holdout groups have changed little over time, continuing the traditional way of life your own people once lived."

"I think these are the people from our children's fairy tales," Kaiya said. "There have always been rumors of their existence, but they're usually considered to be creatures of myth."

"As you can see, they're no myth," Galen stated. He had to repress his smile to keep from insulting Raad. To Galen, this was an amazing discovery. Here he sat in the village of a long-forgotten race. It was as if the pages of one of his history books had suddenly come to life.

"Maybe they're *your* ancestors," Raad said, narrowing his eyes.

"No, the elves have always been elves," Galen replied. "But if I were descended from the Ulihi, I'd be proud."

"Why's that?" the miner asked.

"Because they're an amazing people," the elf replied. "They've managed to stay hidden for centuries, their numbers dwindling but their spirits unbroken. They didn't flinch for a second when they saw us coming."

"You're out of your mind," Raad said.

The argument was interrupted when Tashi stepped inside the hut, two armed warriors close behind her. All three stood the same height as the dwarves, but they were of slighter build than their stocky counterparts. The captives rose to their feet, Galen's head brushing against the top of the hut.

"My name is Tashi," the woman announced. "I am High Priestess of the Ulihi. We have discussed your intrusion upon our hunting grounds," she announced. "We will let two of you go. The third must pay for the transgression."

"What's the price?" Galen asked.

"Death," she replied.

"Peaceful," Raad spat, staring at the elf and shaking his head.

Tashi stared at Galen, her eyes full of curiosity. "Dwarves I know, but you are strange."

"I'm an elf," he replied. "A Westerling Elf of the Vale."

"We have never encountered your people," the priestess replied. "You are a creature of the old songs."

"You mean, I'm a myth to you?" he asked, his head cocked to the side.

Tashi nodded.

"Fascinating," he replied. He had never considered himself to be anything special, but he could fully understand why the Ulihi would not know of his people. The Westerling Elves kept to themselves, rarely leaving their own forest. His own ancestors had inhabited all corners of Nōl'Deron. Now, their descendants populated the forests, but only the Westerling Elves maintained the same physical appearance of the original elves. It was a flattering thought that someone considered him a creature of legend.

"I will not accept you as a sacrifice," Tashi said. Executing a descendant of the Ancients would bring destruction upon her tribe. The old tales spoke vividly of encounters with elves, the benevolent beings who had whispered to the Ulihi the secret of creating fire.

"I appreciate that," Galen said.

"One of you must die," Tashi said, looking to the dwarves.

Knowing that the Ulihi's primitive weapons held no danger for her, Kaiya stated, "Our kinsmen need our help. If you allow my friends to travel in safety to the northern mines, you may execute me if you wish." She stood tall, her chin held high.

Tashi examined the dwarf's face, wondering how she could so easily offer her life for the others. "You are a woman of honor," she stated. "You may go. We will keep the male." Her eyes looked to Raad, who stammered over his protest.

"I will not allow that," Kaiya said. "This man is under my protection."

"Who are you?" Tashi asked.

"My name is Kaiya, and I am a mistress of air magic."

"A sorceress," Tashi said.

"Yes," she replied. "There is a dark presence in these mountains, and I have come to find it before it can do any harm."

"It has already caused great harm," Tashi said, lowering her eyes. "Leave us," she said to the warriors.

They hesitated a moment, but a harsh look from Tashi convinced them to honor her request.

"Darkness has settled upon our tribe, but I do not know its source," she said. "Do you have the ability to sense it?"

Lana Axe

"I do," Kaiya admitted. "I feel no magic among your people, but something is out there, and it's hiding from me."

"Why is that?" Tashi asked.

"Perhaps it is afraid," Kaiya said, uncertain. "Or it is ill-prepared and awaiting the proper time to show itself." She was not so foolish as to believe herself a major threat to an unknown magical entity. Whether it was more or less powerful than she, Kaiya had no way to tell. Only when she met it face to face would she know for certain.

"I have seen dark shadows," Tashi said. "There is evil here, and I cannot contain it."

"I will if I can," Kaiya said.

"You would fight for my people?" Tashi studied Kaiya's face for any hint of deception.

"I would," the sorceress replied.

Instinctively Tashi knew that the dwarf woman was sincere. A silver spark lit in the sorceress's eyes, a message to the priestess that she could be trusted. A gentle breeze moved through the hut, stoking the fire and catching Tashi's eye. The face of her mother flashed before her, fading to that of her sister. The gentle cry of her niece sounded from the village, music to Tashi's ears. This could be the woman who put an end to the Ulihi's curse. Tashi would not let her out of her sight until she knew for certain.

"You are a brave woman," Tashi said. "We are honored to have you among us, and we will accept any help you are willing to give. There are matters we must discuss."

"I'm happy to help you," Kaiya repeated, "but there are dwarves being injured at the mines. I have promised to help them, and I must. Lives are at stake."

"Lives are at stake here as well," Tashi replied. "Many have already been lost."

"What's happened?" Kaiya asked.

"It's as I said before. We are cursed." Tashi's eyes filled with tears. "Too many women are lost in childbirth, and our children no longer survive their first year of life. It is not natural. The gods do nothing to protect us."

"I'm sorry," Kaiya said, the priestess's pain piercing her heart.

"Your magic could save us," Tashi went on. "Will you speak to the Wind God on our behalf?"

"I know of no such being," Kaiya replied. Never in her studies had she encountered anything that could truly be considered a supreme being. There were powerful elementals and powerful wizards, but none had attained the status of a god in her eyes.

"It does not surprise me," the priestess replied, bowing her head. Her own gods had abandoned her, why would the dwarf's gods be any different? "Will you at least meet with my niece and bless her with your magic? She is the only child in our village, and I fear for her."

Looking into Tashi's pleading eyes, Kaiya could not refuse her request. Though she doubted her definition of "blessing" and the Ulihi's were the same, Kaiya would do what she could. "I will," she stated.

"The elf too," Tashi said, nodding toward Galen. "Your people have magic, and it might be of help to my niece."

"I'd be happy to help, and you may call me Galen," he replied. He swallowed hard, knowing that his own magical talents were severely limited, and nearly nonexistent when compared to Kaiya's. But even without magic, Galen was not blind to Tashi's pain. Her yearning to ensure the safety of her niece came from her heart, and the sentiment radiated itself toward the elf. He might be of no help at all, but the least he could do was give Tashi hope.

"This one can stay behind," Tashi said, indicating Raad.

"This one's name is Raad," Kaiya said. "And he goes where I go."

"Very well," Tashi agreed.

The four stepped outside the hut, Tashi pointing toward a woman cradling an infant in her arms. As they moved through the tiny village, every member of the tribe laid eyes on the only visitors they'd witnessed in their lifetimes. Only occasionally did the hunters encounter dwarves, and none had ever been brought back to the village. They were most fascinated by the presence of an elf in their midst, not only for his height but the history he represented. In ancient times his people had been of great service to their own. They looked upon him with wonder.

Visibly frightened, the doula's eyes grew wide. She clutched the infant tightly to her breast, fearing the strangers' approach.

"It's all right," Tashi assured her. "These two have come to help." Tashi reached for her niece, and the doula reluctantly passed the child to her waiting arms.

Presenting the child before Kaiya and Galen, she said, "This is my niece, the daughter of my sister, Annin."

"What's her name?" Galen asked, smiling down at the child.

"She has none." Seeing the elf's confusion, she added, "We do not name a child of this age. She will earn a name after one year."

Kaiya instinctively reached for the child, her gaze fixated on the girl's dark eyes. Tashi hesitated a moment, her heart nearly ceasing to beat. Taking a deep breath, she passed the child to the sorceress.

Cradling the infant, Kaiya closed her eyes and focused her mind to the wind. A glow of silver spread over the child, Tashi taking a step backward at the sight. As quickly as it appeared, the light faded, a silver sparkle remaining momentarily over the child's heart.

"Grow strong, and walk with honor all your days," Kaiya whispered to the child. "May the wind be ever your guide on this journey through life."

The infant looked up at the sorceress and smiled.

Chapter 7

Staring at the infant in her arms, Kaiya beamed with pride. The child squeezed her finger and cooed, warming the sorceress's heart. She had given the child the only blessing she knew, the one her mother had given her when she decided to forgo traditional schooling in favor of learning on her own. Dwarf schools would not teach a child magic, for the simple reason that they had no knowledge of it to pass on. Only elven schools taught such things, but they were too far away from home. Kaiya had learned on her own, and this child could as well. A silver sparkle remained in her eyes, and Kaiya suspected the girl might have an affinity for elemental magic.

Turning to Galen, Kaiya extended the child toward him. "Your turn," she said playfully.

Galen leaned down and took the child as if she were made of porcelain. "Hello, little one," he said softly.

The baby's eyes sparkled with curiosity as she looked upon the elf. Suddenly feeling awkward, Galen's face reddened. He seldom held babies, but somehow it felt natural to him. The tiny bundle was the most precious thing he'd ever seen.

"May the blessings of the elves be upon you," he said, doing his best not to stumble on the words. This was a special moment to the Ulihi, and he didn't want to spoil it.

"With all my heart, I thank you," Tashi said. "Both of you." The arrival of these travelers could not be a coincidence. Had Koli's sacrifice brought this to pass? Or could it be Annin, working to secure her daughter's well-being, even after her death? Tashi took comfort in the thought. Annin had been strong in life, and she would certainly be strong in the life to come.

"You're glowing," Kaiya whispered to Galen.

He continued to stare down at the child, a sideways grin on his face.

"You'll make a wonderful father someday," Kaiya said without thinking. She and Galen had never discussed his desire, or lack thereof, for a family. She had often expressed the sentiment that she did not intend to bear children. He had never argued nor expressed misgivings. His doting over the child only led to further confusion on Kaiya's part.

As if on cue, Galen said, "I think I'd make a better uncle."

A cry ripped through the silent village, startling the visitors as well as the priestess. They looked at each other as the scream sounded again. Something was desperately wrong.

Every male Ulihi grabbed a spear and ran toward the source of the disturbance. The ground shook beneath their feet, but it was no tremor. This was not a constant rumble, but rather a heavy stride. The footsteps approached, the warriors showing no sign of fear.

Frozen in place, Tashi said, "They come for vengeance."

"Who?" Kaiya asked.

"The gods," Tashi replied, her eyes full of terror. She had brought this upon her people.

A form came into view as Kaiya strained to make it out. It was jumbled, loose pieces of rock held together by some force. As it stepped nearer the village, Kaiya couldn't believe her own eyes. Gray stones, amassed more than seven feet high in a rough quadrupedal shape stopped at the edge of the village and rose to its hind legs, preparing for an attack. Though it had no mouth that Kaiya could see, it bellowed a deafening roar.

Turning to Galen, Kaiya said, "Take the child and protect her with your life."

The elf opened his mouth to speak, but Kaiya refused to hear him.

"Keep her safe, and under no circumstances are you to approach this creature or attempt to fight. Do this for me."

With a single nod, Galen clutched the baby to his chest. Glancing at the beast, he turned and ran, the doula following close behind him.

Turning back to Tashi, Kaiya asked, "You've seen these things before?"

"Never," she replied, shaking her head.

The rock monster entered the village on massive stone feet, rattling the Ulihi as they scattered for cover.

Two warriors charged forward, spears in hand. Their war cries echoed in Kaiya's ears as she watched them fall, crushed by the weight of the beast, who continued forward without a thought for the lives it had taken.

Raad darted forward as the creature passed, grabbing a spear from one of the fallen warriors. Running to join the other men, they positioned themselves into a battle formation. Standing behind them were the majority of the village's women, the warriors shouting for them to flee. To their credit, most of the women refused. They grabbed loose rocks and burning torches, ready to defend their homes. Only the oldest among them fled to safety.

Tashi ripped the bottom from her staff, dropping the top to the ground. Kaiya looked at her in confusion until she realized what the priestess actually held. Placing the bottom end of the staff to her lips, she blew inside it, sending a dart speeding toward the rock beast. It glanced off the creature's armored hide, causing it no harm.

As the men began their charge toward the beast, Kaiya readied her hands. Silver sparks swirled upon her fingers, the wind racing at her back. Focusing her mind to the enemy, she struggled against its weight to hold it solidly in place.

Seeing their enemy struggle against the wind, Raad and the warriors charged. With a grunt, Raad thrust the spear between the rocks that made up one of the monster's legs. The force of the blow sent a shattering pain through his arm, his shoulder crunching and wrenching itself at an odd angle. Crying out in agony, he dropped the spear and grasped his shoulder with his other hand. Unable to shift the injured arm back into its correct position, he stumbled out of the way, cursing.

The rest of the warriors continued the onslaught, breaking their spears upon the rocks. The creature remained in position, completely unaffected by their weapons. The women threw their rocks, hoping to knock pieces away from the creature to weaken it. But the rocks glanced off without harming the beast. Fire had no effect as they lobbed their torches toward it. One succeeded in lighting fire to a hut, sending warriors and women alike scrambling to contain the flames before they could spread across the village.

Kaiya held her breath, her strength waning. The creature's weight was immense, forcing her to expend a vast supply of magic to restrain it. Dropping to one knee, the sorceress began to sweat. Sensing the beast's mind, she knew it had but one purpose—to destroy.

The rock beast swayed and struggled, freeing its feet enough to move a few inches. Three women fled from beneath it, one of them crashing into Kaiya as she struggled to maintain her focus. Losing her concentration, the sorceress faltered, and the beast charged forward unimpeded.

The woman helped Kaiya to her feet, both terror and sympathy in her eyes. The sorceress attempted to catch her breath, but there was no time to spare. The beast crashed into an unoccupied hut, smashing it with a single step. It swiped a massive arm at a second hut, toppling it as if it were no more than a pile of leaves.

The warriors reformed their ranks, determined to continue the fight. Swinging its head around, the beast focused its attention on them. It pawed a foreleg against the ground, kicking up dirt and snow. An angry growl escaped the beast as it reared onto its hind legs, preparing for another attack.

The warriors stood their ground, but Kaiya knew they would not survive. Squeezing her eyes shut, she summoned the wind above her, focusing her magic to the sky. Dark clouds swirled above her, a burst of thunder splitting the air. Her violet hair blew violently on the wind, scratching at her face. With a single blast of wind, she knocked the Ulihi backward, sending them tumbling to safety. Throwing open her eyes, a bright flash of silver erupted from them, calling the lightning from the sky. In a single strike, it blasted the stone beast, shattering its rear half into hundreds of pieces. Exhausted, she collapsed on the ground, her head slumped over her knees.

The warriors wasted no time getting back to their feet. This was the opportunity they needed. Leaping onto the creature as it writhed in agony, they tore at the rocks until they managed to wrest a few from their proper position. The beast tumbled, its form too weakened to maintain itself. With a cry of victory, the Ulihi stood over their kill.

Tashi raced to Kaiya's side, finding her unconscious. Gently she rolled the dwarf onto her back and brushed her hair away from her face. Leaning down, she pressed her ear to the woman's chest. To Tashi's relief, the sorceress was still breathing, her heartbeat strong.

Opening her eyes, Kaiya bolted upright, a silver sheen disappearing from her face. Her eyes shot to the fallen beast, and she whispered a word of thanks to the wind.

"You have saved us," Tashi said, extending her hand to Kaiya.

The sorceress gladly took it, pulling herself back to her feet. As she stood, she felt eyes upon her. The presence had returned. Its force was strong, focusing its will upon her. A great malice entered her heart, burning throughout her body. This was a force of pure evil, and she had angered it by defending these people. Whoever had sent the beast was taking notes, and the next one would not go down so easily.

Not that Kaiya had found the battle easy by any means. Her head spun from the effort, and she felt as if she hadn't slept for a week. The muscles in her arms ached from fatigue and overuse, and her legs were jelly beneath her. These things she hid well, knowing that she could not let the true enemy see any sign of weakness in her. Conventional weapons weren't going to banish this threat, and she knew of no other in the mountains who could lend magical aid.

The images from her vision flashed once again in her mind. It was imperative she continue her journey higher into the mountains. Her final destination would not be the painite mines.

"Are you injured?" Tashi asked.

The sorceress shook her head. "Tired is all," she said. "You?"

"I am well, but others have fallen," Tashi replied. Her eyes looked to the fallen warriors, whose bodies were being wrapped in blankets.

Galen rose from his position behind a boulder, the infant cradled in his arms. The doula, who had pressed herself close to him to further shield the child, rose as well, with a simple nod to a job well done. Together they reentered the village.

Hearing footsteps behind her, Tashi spun around. Her heart leapt to see the elf still clutching her niece. "I thank you for protecting this child," she said to him, bowing slightly. She inclined her head to the doula, who reached for the child.

Before passing the child to her caretaker, Galen leaned down and kissed her forehead. As he handed her over, he said, "She didn't cry or make a single sound."

"That is because she is Ulihi," Tashi said, holding her head high. "She knows when danger is near."

"Danger will return," Kaiya said. "We must continue on our journey."

Raad made his way toward them, still clutching at his dislocated shoulder.

"This man is injured," Tashi said, a line of worry wrinkling her brow. Reaching out for him, she said, "You risked your life for my people. You are a warrior."

The miner swayed and pursed his lips. "I wouldn't go that far," he said. "I did more damage to myself than that monster." To Kaiya, he asked, "What was that thing?"

"I don't know," she replied, "but I intend to find out."

Examining the dwarf's injured shoulder, the priestess said, "This will have to be reset. It will hurt, but only for a moment."

Without another word, she yanked on his arm, doubling him over in surprise. Pressing her bare foot against his armpit, she wrenched the arm back into place. A sickening crunch sounded, and a sharp pain shot through Raad's body. For a moment he thought he might lose consciousness, but as soon as the pain had started, it vanished.

"I will wrap that in place for you," she said, turning away and dashing inside a hut. She returned seconds later with a strip of cloth which she fashioned into a sling. "That will feel better in a few days."

His arm immobilized and feeling much better, Raad said, "Thank you, ma'am." His eyes scanned the snow for his fallen backpack, his taste buds desperate for a sip of ale. Looking at his arm, he said, "I don't suppose I'll be able to carry my pack."

"I'll get it," Galen offered. Jogging across the village he retrieved the dwarf's belongings and adjusted the straps to fit his own frame. Returning to his companions, he said, "It's the least I can do for a warrior."

Raad rolled his eyes. "Let me at that ale," he said.

"Later," Kaiya stated firmly. "We need to get going. I'm ready to find out what that creature was, and what it wanted from these people."

"How can you protect us if you aren't here?" Tashi asked. "I implore you to stay."

"I cannot," Kaiya said. "Whatever sent that thing is a threat to us all, not only your tribe. A vision has sent me higher into the mountains, to the very summit perhaps. But first I must get to the mines, and we've already gone off-course."

Slowly nodding, the priestess said, "I understand. There is a passage through these mountains that will take you to the mines by nightfall. There is no need for you to return to the path where we found you."

"If you can give us directions, I'd be most grateful," Kaiya replied.

"It is a difficult trail," Tashi said. "I will come with you as your guide."

Raad looked the priestess over, making note of her slender build and bare feet. "There are avalanches and other dangers up there," he said. "I don't think it's safe for you."

"I can look out for myself," she replied, a fire in her eyes.

"I don't doubt that," the dwarf responded.

"Will you allow me to travel with you?" she asked Kaiya.

"You may," the sorceress replied. "We're grateful for your help." Time was of the essence, and the priestess could save them a lot of it.

"Aren't you needed here?" Galen asked, thinking of the baby. "Your niece?"

"The doula knows more of infant care than I do," she replied. "Without my sister, there is no one here who needs me." A pain shot through Tashi's heart at the thought of Annin. The hole left by her absence would never heal. "I would also like answers," she added. "This beast has attacked my people, and I would bring justice to its master."

"As would I," Kaiya said, admiring the priestess's strong convictions.

"Please don't go, Tashi," the doula said, her dark eyes pleading.

"I must," she replied. "I would make this a better world for this child." She took the infant in her arms and held her close to her heart. "Know always that I love you, and that your mother loved you more than life itself." With tears in her eyes, she handed the girl back to the doula. "Be well," she said. Taking her position in front of the others, she led them northward. Pausing only a moment, she looked back toward the village. *They are safe now.*

Chapter 8

Stepping with ease over the stony terrain, Tashi led the group northward. Kaiya walked at the priestess's side, with Galen and Raad close behind. Obstacles hidden in the snow proved no problem for Tashi, who moved as lightly as a bird. The dwarves, however, tripped frequently, Raad cursing with each bruise to his toes. Being an elf, Galen struggled little. A heightened sense of balance and nimble feet gave him an edge over his dwarf companions.

Tashi pointed forward. "The path is just ahead," she said. "It is uneven with many jagged rocks."

"So watch our steps or we might twist an ankle," Raad finished for her.

"Yes," Tashi said. "Dwarves walk too heavily upon the land."

"A heavy step means your foot is in a solid hold," the miner countered.

"But here you will not be able to see what is beneath the piled snow," she replied. "It's best to step lightly to avoid injury."

"Take her advice," Kaiya said, reaching for the wind. Magic could lighten her step, and perhaps she could provide assistance to Raad too. As long as the air around her continued to move, she would not lack for power. Still, she would use very little. It was best to be at full strength should another stone monster appear.

As they reached the intended path, the group saw no change in the terrain. It was strewn with snow, the tops of gray rocks jutting upward, whispering a warning to the travelers.

"We don't come this way often," Tashi said. "Once we traveled great distances, but now these paths are rarely used."

Raad stared at the priestess with uncertainty. "You sure it's the right one?"

"It will take us to your mines," she promised. Stepping ahead, she pointed out a narrow clearing that existed among the rocks. It was far from straight, but it would provide safe passage.

Single file the travelers moved on, stumbling each time they lost the path—all except Tashi, who had no trouble finding where to step. The clearing was made for small feet, not the wide boots of the dwarves.

The path grew steeper as they trudged ahead, their legs already aching with exertion. Several times Kaiya nearly slipped, forcing her to put more effort into her magic. Raad seemed to notice the improvement, and patted her on the back.

Cresting the hill, the travelers looked upon a scene of true beauty. The rock-strewn path gave way to a grassy clearing, powdered with the purest white snow. Evergreens stretched out before them, their rich green needles peppered with white snow.

"It's beautiful," Kaiya commented, her gray eyes full of wonder.

"This is how our mountains looked before the miners came," Tashi said.

"Now hold on, missy," Raad said, waving his good arm. "We haven't done any damage anywhere. We build settlements and dig deep. That doesn't include destroying any landscapes."

"Doesn't it?" Tashi asked. "Your kind do not respect the land or those who dwell there."

"There are only two mines at this elevation," Raad replied knowingly.

"In this area, yes," Tashi said. "But the mountains are vast, and my people have been driven out of many areas. Once we were nomads, traveling throughout the region. Now we move only to avoid the mines."

"That isn't our doing," Raad said. "Unless your kind used to live down in the holes, we haven't disturbed your land."

The heat rising to her face, Tashi replied, "For millennia my people dwelt here. Our numbers were great, our children strong. Our sacred sites have disappeared, fallen to the hammers and axes of the dwarves."

Grunting his disagreement, Raad said, "I've never heard of any mining operation running people off their land. Those sites are scouted thoroughly, and anything that looks like it'll pose an expensive problem is a deal-breaker. We want ore, not trouble with the natives."

"You take more than you need, and you leave only destruction," the priestess shot back.

Galen spoke up, attempting to soften the argument. "It's possible that a nomadic people wouldn't have been home when scouting was completed," he suggested. "No one would know there had been an intrusion until the tribe returned."

"And we cannot stand against your kind in a fight, so we must go wherever we can find," Tashi said. "Soon there will be nowhere to go." Not that it mattered much. With no children surviving to adulthood, the Ulihi would soon be extinct. The sentiment found its way to her tongue, but she swallowed it, refusing to admit defeat in front of the miner.

"You make a valid point, Galen," Kaiya cut in. "It is not unlike my people to think only of themselves." To Tashi, she said, "Until we met, I had no idea your people existed. You were a bedtime story of a people long gone from this world. We can't protect what we don't know exists, but I agree we should have looked harder. I apologize for that." What more could she say? She could not change the past, but it was still possible to shape the future.

After a moment of thought, Kaiya said, "As soon as I return, I'll speak to leadership about protecting tribal lands. It shouldn't be too difficult to convince them." Due to the small size of the Ulihi tribe, they didn't need much room. In addition, the land they inhabited was not where the dwarves preferred to dwell. But the men in charge could be stubborn when they saw something they wanted, and the glint of gold or some other ore could drive them to break any treaty signed with the Ulihi. In all likelihood, Kaiya would have to take her argument all the way to the king. Only his refusal to allow the building of new mines would put a stop to the incursion.

Her tone softening, Tashi said, "It is good of you to do this. I hope you will succeed." Glancing over at Raad, she said, "I do not blame you personally. You did not build the mines, and you did not steal Ulihi lands."

"Err, thanks," the miner replied.

"But you work for them, and you take from the land what should be left undisturbed. I wonder what your gods think of that."

"My gods are made of stone," he jibed. "What I do honors them."

"Is this true?" the priestess asked.

"It's true that some dwarves worship the stone," Kaiya explained. "I'm a little skeptical about Raad. I think he only worships the cask."

The miner laughed heartily. "You got me there."

"As for myself, I put my faith in the magic around me," Kaiya went on. "The element that fuels my power and gives me strength is all I need."

"My people believe that the gods inhabit all things," Tashi said. "We have many of them, too many perhaps. Some have been long forgotten." She didn't know why, but the thought filled her with sorrow. It was possible her people had chosen poorly when it came to the gods. Could the forgotten ones have healed the children? She would never know.

"Fairy tales," Raad grumbled.

"How do you mean?" Galen asked.

"A god of this and a god of that," he said. "All fairy stories. Just like my old Gran when she told me about the mountain sprites." He smirked, looking over at Tashi. "She used to make up stories of little people who ran around naked in the snow."

"Seems that fairy tale was true," Galen pointed out.

"I suppose so," the miner replied.

"We don't walk naked," Tashi stated, "but we don't need the heavy clothing you wear. We have lived among the snow-covered peaks for millennia and are well-suited to it."

The group circled around a narrow ledge, slowly making their way around an unmovable boulder. Time and wind had smoothed it, the snow refusing to cling to its polished surface. Tashi rubbed her hand along its cold exterior.

"These smooth stones bring good luck," she said. "Touch it as you pass."

Kaiya did as the priestess bid, as did Galen. Seeing that the other two were participating, Raad reluctantly reached out his hand. It was likely nonsense, but miners could be superstitious as well. Rubbing one's hands with dirt was essential before digging commenced. There was no reason for it, but everyone did it just the same. This act was no different.

"Tell me about yourself, Tashi," Galen said. "I've read of your people, but what's written in old tomes isn't necessarily the real story. I'd love to hear what life is like for you."

Giving the elf a sideways glance, Tashi tried to decide whether he was sincere. Making note of the slight smile on his lips, and his curious eyes, she concluded that his desire to learn was genuine.

"I am a high priestess," she began. "I have many duties among my people. Most important is to speak to the gods on behalf of the tribe, and to administer blessings."

"Do you use magic?" the elf asked.

She considered the question a moment. "Not in the way that Kaiya does," she finally said. "I perform rituals as taught to me by my mother." She looked down at her feet.

Noticing her pained expression, Galen asked, "What happened to her?"

"She died giving life to my dear sister, Annin," Tashi replied, tears spilling from her eyes. "And now Annin is also gone, her life given for her child as well."

"I'm sorry," Galen said.

"I was powerless to prevent it," she went on. "And more will surely die. It is my failing."

"You couldn't possibly be responsible," the elf replied.

"I am the one who implores the blessing of the gods," she said. "But the gods have abandoned me and all my people." Her sorrow turned to anger, her voice growing louder, as if issuing a challenge. "Maybe they have died or found someone else to amuse them. Maybe our suffering amuses them. Who can say? Why else would they allow our children to die?"

"There are many skilled healers among my people," Galen said. "When I return to the Vale, I will find the best among them and send them to aid you. I have no doubt one of them will find a cure."

"Your offer is kind," she replied, "but this is not a disease of the body. This is a curse of the gods, a true work of evil. Your healers can do nothing."

"I'm still going to speak with them," he promised.

Tashi nodded, but the words did not give her hope. She had already made the mistake of calling upon darkness to replace the missing light, and it had ended in disaster. No elf medicine would bring the gods back to the Ulihi, and Tashi had failed in her position as their spiritual leader. The image of her niece crept back into her mind, and her heart ached anew. The sorceress had to know a way to save the child. Magic was a tool of the gods, and it could be used to defy their will. If the gods planned to take Annin's daughter, maybe Kaiya could stop them.

"What is your reason for traveling to the mines?" Tashi asked. "Why do they need your magic?" Had the gods found a way to punish the miners as well as the Ulihi?

"There have been avalanches, and people are getting hurt," Kaiya said. "They sent Raad to fetch me to see if I could put a stop to it."

"They should be used to such things," Tashi said. "An avalanche is not an uncommon thing in these mountains." Her voice was full of disappointment. This was not the work of the gods, only nature.

"I also had a vision," Kaiya added.

Those words piqued Tashi's interest. "What did you see?" she asked eagerly.

"I sensed a presence, and I saw myself high in the mountains," Kaiya said. "Then I fell down into the heart of the mountain."

"That is a powerful vision," the priestess whispered. "Do you know who it was that you sensed?"

"A great mind," the sorceress replied. "It was strong, powerful, and it definitely has an agenda. That's why I'm traveling to the mines. I believe the avalanches there, the tremors in my own hometown, and my vision are all related."

Swallowing hard, Tashi wondered if the demons she had unleashed could be the cause of it all. Her attempt to enlist the help of the dead god might have affected more than just the Ulihi. Once evil was unleashed, it was difficult to contain. It could wreak havoc wherever it pleased unless checked by a higher power. Tashi had no true magic with which to combat it, nor did any member of her tribe.

Looking the sorceress up and down, she attempted to measure her proficiency. Would this dwarf be strong enough? Tashi could only hope so. If Kaiya failed, there might not be time to seek out another. The Ulihi would be doomed, as would the dwarves.

The path grew wider as it twisted around a bend. The snow here was deeper, reaching past the dwarves' ankles, and it showed no signs of disturbance by animal or otherwise. It lay perfectly smooth and even, a thin layer of melt forming on its top under the rays of the afternoon sun.

As the gap spread out, so did the weary companions. Their leg muscles ached from their steep-angle trek, but this area was primarily flat. The ground crunched slightly beneath their feet, a layer of gravel paving the way. Travel would be less challenging, at least for a while.

Looking into the distance, Kaiya could not resist a brief pause to admire the view. A gentle mist settled throughout the mountains on her right, as they spread endlessly into the shadows. A land wholly unspoiled by the touch of the dwarves, her heart yearned to explore it. This, however, was not the time. Her vision played over in her mind, telling her that there were other sights still to be seen.

"I think it's getting colder," Galen commented, pulling his cloak nearer his skin. He glanced skyward, puzzled at the drop in temperature. This should have been the warmest time of day, especially judging by the thin layer of melting ice atop the snowfall.

Grabbing Tashi's arm, Kaiya stopped her from going any farther. She held up a hand for the others to stop as well before turning her ear to the wind, a voice wafting clearly toward her.

"Something is out there," she said.

Chapter 9

"You see something?" Raad asked, squinting his eyes and craning his neck. Whatever Kaiya was seeing, the miner was not.

"I didn't see it," the sorceress replied. "I felt it." Tuning her mind to the snow-covered path before them, she searched for whatever was watching. This was entirely different from the presence she had sensed before. This creature was also angry, but it was far less powerful.

"There!" Galen shouted, pointing toward the tree line. Outlined against the green boughs and powdery snow, the shape of a face came into view, its dark hair and eyes unmistakable against the backdrop.

"I don't see anything," Tashi said, still straining to see.

"I thought I did, but it's gone," Raad said.

"Not gone," Kaiya said. "She's moving closer." The presence was distinctly female, both angry and woeful. *Who are you?* she projected with her mind.

No answer.

Trying again, the sorceress sent her message along the wind. *Who are you? How did you come to this pass? Do you need help?*

Silence.

"I see her!" Tashi shouted, pointing to a new location. The eyes stared out at the travelers, a hint of longing written within them.

Shutting her eyes, Kaiya waited, her ears hearing nothing but the wind. Finally, a voice drifted softly along an icy breeze.

Who am I? One who is lost. You are the help I seek.

Kaiya's eyes shot open, the woman's words echoing in her ears. There was malice behind them, her true intent uncertain.

"She's moving toward us," Galen said.

Looking straight ahead, the image of a woman in a flowing white robe appeared before them. She floated above the snow, no visible feet touching the ground. Her body was transparent, her form barely discernable in the distance. Softly, slowly, she moved toward the travelers.

"A yukona," Tashi said, her voice cracking.

"Explain," Kaiya replied, keeping her eyes focused on the apparition.

"She is an ancient spirit," the priestess said. "The soul of one who died in this pass in a snowstorm or avalanche, and she has remained trapped."

"What does she want?" Galen asked, fearing the answer.

"A host," Tashi replied. "She craves a mortal body that she might walk the earth once more."

"Well, she can't have mine," Raad said, readying himself for a fight.

"I doubt she'd want it," Galen replied. "She probably wants Kaiya or Tashi."

"Male or female doesn't matter to her," Tashi explained. "She is angry, and she will kill to get what her heart desires."

"Do you know how to stop her?" Kaiya asked, fearing the answer.

"She can't be stopped," Tashi replied. "We must outrun her."

At those words the group proceeded forward at a brisk pace, but they did not run. The yukona's movements were too unpredictable, and running could easily land them straight in her clutches.

Fewer than a hundred feet ahead, Tashi, who was in the lead, slammed into an unseen barrier, landing hard on her back. Kaiya helped her to her feet and placed a palm against the invisible wall.

"She's erected some kind of shield," she announced. "We'll have to find a way around it."

The group spread out, each of them running their hands along the barrier, searching for an opening.

"Over here," Raad called.

The others joined him, still guiding themselves with their hands. The wall was now on both sides of them, a narrow hallway of magical barriers forcing them toward the trees.

"She's funneling us," Kaiya muttered, her displeasure obvious.

The path grew narrower, forcing them into single file. Kaiya took the lead, her eyes glowing with silver magic. A piercing shriek sliced through their ears, their hands instinctively reaching up to cover them.

Anger rose in the sorceress, the magical barrier preventing her full contact with the wind. Summoning her magical stores, she turned her palms outward, blasting energy at the barrier. She could sense it weakening, the air surrounding it forcing the walls outward. Another blast collapsed the shield, silver sparks raining where the barrier had stood.

An ethereal face appeared before Tashi, close enough she could have reached up and touched it. In an instant, it disappeared, leaving no clue as to where it might have gone.

"Run!" the priestess shouted.

This time, the others obeyed. Dashing away from the trees, they ran for the center of the gap. If the yukona wanted them near the trees, they would stay as far from them as possible. Running through the clearing, all eyes ahead, they attempted to outrun their hidden enemy. Raad lagged behind the others, but the touch of an unseen hand on his shoulder prompted him to quicken his pace.

A second mournful wail cut through the frigid air with a force great enough to knock the travelers off their feet. The yukona hadn't finished with these invaders. She needed one of them to stay behind, to give her what she craved.

Kaiya rolled to her feet, her hands lit with silver sparks. Summoning the wind, she allowed her mind to travel on it, searching for the apparition. A single strand of dark hair revealed itself, floating only a few feet above Tashi.

"Stay down!" the sorceress shouted.

Tashi obeyed, laying low to the ground. Kaiya unleashed an energy blast over the priestess's head, hitting the yukona in her midsection. The specter flew backward, doubling over in surprise. Regaining her senses, her eyes flashed with anger. With blind fury, she flew at the sorceress, her clawed fingers aimed for the kill.

Wasting no time, Kaiya raised her hands to the sky, her hair swirling on an upward draft. The whirling air intensified, lifting her feet slightly off the ground. Redirecting the wind, she launched it forward, catching the yukona midair. The creature lurched sideways, desperately clawing at the air, but to no avail.

Her eyes flashing silver, Kaiya sent the cyclone along with the specter hurtling toward the trees, rattling the boughs and forcing them aside. A shriek sounded in the distance as the yukona was carried farther and farther away, fading into a distant memory.

"Let's get out of here," Kaiya said, dropping her hands to her sides.

"Will she come after us?" Galen asked as the group started to run.

"I don't want to find out," Raad answered.

In the distance, Kaiya could still sense the yukona. She was angry and bitter, but she was not in pursuit. The sorceress did not know whether such a creature could be physically injured, but it didn't matter. If she and her friends made it away from the woods, they would likely be safe. The yukona was best left to her own misery.

Ignoring their rumbling stomachs and aching feet, the four of them moved on, hoping to put a great distance between themselves and the apparition. It was hours before they decided to pause for a rest and have a few bites to eat. The sun was already moving behind the mountain, and the light was beginning to fade.

Passing around what was left of her food, Kaiya urged her companions to eat quickly. "We need to reach the mines by nightfall."

"It might be best to make camp here," Raad suggested. "The sun disappears early up here."

It was sound advice, but Kaiya had had enough. And she wouldn't risk the return of the yukona. "It isn't safe here," she said. "We can't stay."

Not up for an argument, Raad nodded. "How much farther, do you think?"

"We will arrive tonight," Tashi said, "but not before dark."

"Then let's get moving," the miner replied.

As they returned to their feet, the ground trembled beneath them. The sound was quiet at first, but crescendoed into a thundering roar.

"Another quake?" Raad asked.

Tashi shook her head. "Avalanche!" she cried, staring upward. Snow slid along the steep embankment to their left. "Take cover!"

Their best bet for cover was a series of large boulders, which they quickly darted behind. The falling ice and snow crashed around them, losing speed as it crossed the gap and slid out of sight over the edge. Kaiya risked moving from safety to observe the peak.

"It's finished," she announced. "We can consider ourselves lucky."

"But what caused it?" Galen asked. "Will it happen again?" There might not always be a boulder to hide behind if they continued their climb.

"That is nature," Tashi said. "It happens often." She could not remember how many hundreds of avalanches she had witnessed in her lifetime. One of her duties as High Priestess was to ensure her village was protected from such things. It did not require spells or incantations, or even the blessing of the gods. It was a matter of simple geography, knowing the lay of the land.

"Kaiya?" Galen asked, awaiting confirmation.

"I sense no magic involved," Kaiya stated, easing the elf's tension. "Let's keep going."

Racing the setting sun, they pressed on at a fast pace. Landmarks became scarce, the landscape becoming barren, save for the ever-present rocks and snow. Luckily the surface was relatively smooth, allowing them to move faster than expected.

When the sun finally moved behind the mountain, only a pinkish glow remained to light the way. Raad grumbled, "I hope one of you can see in the dark."

"Lend me your staff," Kaiya said to Tashi.

Tashi handed it over, one eyebrow raised high. The dwarf must be tiring if she needed a stick to lean on.

Waving a hand over the top of the staff, a silver-pink glow came over the ornamental goat skull. Lifting it high, she said, "This will light the way."

"How?" Tashi asked, not understanding what she had witnessed. "How are you doing that?"

"I'm pulling the leftover light from the sunset and channeling it into the staff," the sorceress explained. "When the sun is gone, I'll use the moon's light. Don't worry, it won't actually burn the staff." It was a simple spell that Kaiya used often for a variety of different purposes. Pulling light and heat were one of the first lessons a sorceress learned when she began her studies. For anyone magically inclined, it came easiest of any spell.

"Amazing," Tashi commented, still marveling at the light emitted by her own staff. "May I?" she asked, reaching for it.

"Of course," Kaiya said, passing it back to her.

Tashi inspected the glowing skull, its eyes projecting the path ahead. "Can you teach me?" she wondered.

"I'm not sure," Kaiya answered. She could perceive no magic in Tashi, but that didn't mean it was impossible. However, Kaiya had never tried to teach someone a spell, whether they were born with magic or not. Without formal training herself, she had never encountered other students. She simply didn't know if someone born without magic could ever be able to channel it.

Galen saved her the trouble. "This type of spell uses inborn magic," he explained. "Those who can cast it usually figure it out early on, sometimes to their surprise."

"What do you mean?" Tashi asked.

"Take me, for example. All elves can cast a few spells, this one included. But I am no sorcerer, and I have no talent for magic. That doesn't mean I can't learn, but someone who is trained can perform far-more-intense spells."

"Does that mean I can or I can't learn?" Tashi didn't understand the elf's meaning.

"You'd have to be tested," he replied. "But if you have no natural ability, you'll probably never learn elemental magic. If you weren't born with a magical store, you can't grow one." He paused a moment. "Though I have read of creatures such as dragons imbuing their powers upon others. Maybe it's not impossible. And, of course, there are other forms of magic that don't require a magical store. Those spells require intense training."

Never having encountered a dragon, Tashi knew receiving its blessing was an impossibility for her. She hadn't shown any special abilities as a child, so it was unlikely she could learn Kaiya's style of magic. The elements would no more obey her than the gods. It was another shortcoming, but one she could live with. She was no better or worse than she had been. In Kaiya she had found a magical ally, and that would have to be enough.

Raising the staff high, Tashi lit the way ahead. "We are close," she announced. Straight ahead was a cliffside, blocking their path to the mines. Pausing before it, she said, "Now we climb."

"With one arm?" Raad asked. The cliff was not terribly high, but in his injured state, it would be impossible for him to climb it. There were four handholds he would need to grasp as he ascended, and letting go of one to grasp the next would mean plummeting back to the bottom.

Standing next to the cliff, Galen saw an easy solution. "I'll go up first and pull you," he said. The cliff was only two feet above his head. Once he reached the top, he would still have enough leverage to pull the dwarf, provided he was able to stand on the lowest ledge.

Grasping the uppermost handhold, the elf easily pulled himself to the top. Kneeling down, he extended an arm to his companions below. Kaiya and Tashi moved in to brace Raad, easing him onto the lower footholds. Holding his breath, Raad grasped the elf's arm while the women pushed from below. Before he could panic, he was back on solid ground. He nodded his thanks to the elf.

Galen offered a hand to the ladies as well, pulling each of them to the safety of the plateau. Satisfied with a job well done, he readjusted his pack and dusted the snow from his knees.

"Pretty handy to have someone like you around," Raad said, grinning.

"Glad I could help," the elf replied.

From this vantage point, the travelers could clearly make out the ocean in the distance. Lit by moonlight, its shining surface sparkled before them. Massive blocks of ice moved up and down as if they drew breath, rocked by the rolling waves beneath them. Birds called in the distance, singing a tribute to the night sky.

"The breathing ice," Tashi said. "Ulihi hunters sometimes travel here to hunt seals, though not as much as when I was a child. Goats are more plentiful and closer to home."

"The view alone is worth the travel," Galen said, his eyes filled with wonder.

Strange sounds in the distance drew their attention away from the sea, their ears straining to make out the noise.

"Voices," Tashi whispered, wondering who might be near.

"Echoes," Raad corrected. "That'll be the miners."

Sure enough, the mining camp became visible as they moved atop the next hill. Ahead of them in the darkness, lanterns shone, and dark figures moved about.

"Home sweet home," the miner said, relieved to be back.

"No," Kaiya said. "That's no mining camp."

Chapter 10

"Of course it's a mining camp," Raad countered. "This is where we've been trying to get to."

Kaiya gaped as she looked ahead at the camp before her. "This is a city," she said. The camp stretched on for miles, going far beyond her line of sight. Far larger than the village near her farm, this was the largest mining operation she had ever seen.

Its existence gave credence to Tashi's words about dwarves encroaching on her tribal lands. All the remaining Ulihi could fit easily into a quarter of this city. The priestess had accused the dwarves of greed, and judging by the size of this encampment, the statement seemed to ring true. At least in this instance, it looked as if they'd taken more than they needed.

Every home was constructed of wood and stone, not the temporary tent dwellings that normally went along with mining life. Clearly the dwarves planned to stay permanently, which meant more settlements popping up between here and Kaiya's village weren't out of the question. Shortening supply lines would save them money, and that could spell trouble for the Ulihi. They might soon be losing more hunting ground.

"We might as well get settled," Raad said. "Foreman Daro always goes to bed early, so you won't be meeting with him tonight. He'll be up at dawn, though, so you won't have to wait much longer."

Kaiya sighed and ground her teeth. She was anxious to find out exactly why Daro had summoned her. There was more to the story than Raad had revealed, and she was impatient to learn the missing parts. "Maybe I should wake him," she said. "He did ask you to fetch me."

"Let the man rest," Raad said, waving a dismissive hand. "We can enjoy ourselves at one of the taverns."

"One of?" Galen asked.

"We have six," Raad replied, grinning.

Tashi shook her head. "Why do you need so many?"

"We've got a large operation going on here, in case you hadn't noticed," he replied. "There's lots of mouths to feed and water."

Uninterested in revelry, Kaiya asked, "Does this place have an inn?"

"Nope," Raad replied, "but you can have a spot in the bunkhouse. It's meant for temporary workers, but it's empty this time of year. You'll have a little privacy."

Resigning herself to an uncomfortable night, Kaiya said, "Lead the way."

Motioning for the others to follow, Raad led them into the mining camp. They passed by two taverns, filled to the brim with sloshed miners. The ones who were still partly sober took notice of the travelers, mainly Tashi and Galen. They stood out in this place, even in the dark.

Emboldened by a few drinks, one man stepped in Tashi's path and placed a hand on her beaded collar. "What have we got here?" he asked, his gaze tracing the lines of her figure.

"This is the woman who will break your hand if you don't keep it off her," Tashi warned, her features stern.

The dwarf withdrew his hand and wiped it against his chest. "Fiery, aren't you," he commented.

"Get back to your drink," Raad demanded, stepping between Tashi and the dwarf.

The man peered around Raad, considering whether he wanted to obey. One look at Kaiya, and he decided he'd best go back inside. Without another word, he disappeared into the tavern crowd.

"What did you do to him?" Raad asked.

"Not a thing," Kaiya replied, a crooked smile on her lips. A flash of silver in her eyes was all it had taken to scare the inebriated miner. Dwarves rarely encountered any sort of magic, so having it stand in front of them could be rather intimidating.

As they continued through the city, Kaiya made note of a small school. "There are children here?" she asked.

"Yes, ma'am," Raad replied. Seeing her confusion, he added, "You can't expect men to live way up here without bringing their families along."

Raising a family this far from dwarf civilization seemed strange to her. Shrugging it off, she decided it was no stranger than her own upbringing. Never having fit in with the other children, she had chosen to separate herself from them. At least these kids had each other.

Crossing a narrow alleyway, Kaiya glimpsed the movement of a cat, its eyes shining in the dim light. The back of her throat tingled, a salty taste filling her mouth. Tilting her head, she sniffed at the wind.

"Barracks are to your left," Raad announced, pointing. "Door's unlocked, so help yourself."

"There's magic here," the sorceress announced, her head lifted high. "This way," she said, following the scent.

The others followed, curious to discover the source. Drawing more energy into Tashi's staff, Kaiya illuminated the darkness surrounding them. She moved away from the city, where no lamps were burning.

"Where are you going?" Raad wondered. Traveling outside the camp at night was unsafe, but there was little chance he could change the sorceress's mind. Especially with only one usable arm, he couldn't hope to force her back toward safety. "There are wild beasts in these mountains, you know," he said, attempting to warn her.

Not listening, Kaiya continued to follow the scent burning in her nostrils. "Here," she said, stopping near a pile of rubble. It stretched on for several feet, loose rocks combined with packed ice. A faint trail remained visible where the stones had slid to their current position.

"What happened here?" Tashi asked. Placing her foot against the fallen stones, a shiver ran through her body. Was this the magic Kaiya spoke of?

Kneeling on tired knees, Kaiya ran her fingers over the rubble, a silver light trailing behind them. "These are the remains of an avalanche," she announced. A nearly undetectable energy remained, causing her fingers to tingle.

"So what?" Raad asked. "This part didn't do any damage. It's the debris closer to the mine that caused the most harm."

"I understand that," she replied, her patience wearing thin. "This may have done no damage, but there is magic behind it."

"What does that mean?" Tashi wondered. "Is that the cause of any avalanche?" This discovery had her questioning what she had believed was a natural occurrence.

Lowering herself, Kaiya laid her head sideways upon the rocks, the searing cold finding its way through her cheek and into her throat. Behind it was a distinct presence—unseen, unheard. A sensation of falling through the earth flashed in her mind, prompting her to pull away from the rocks. Sitting up with a jolt, she said, "This was not the work of nature. Not at all."

The fine hairs on the back of Tashi's neck stood up, a shiver racing along her spine. *What have I done?* From the corner of her eye, she thought she saw a shadow move. When none of the others acknowledged it, she questioned whether it was her imagination.

"Who caused it, then?" Galen asked. Only an earth mage of incredible power could summon an avalanche. Unless there were darker forces at work—ancient ones.

Tashi looked away, avoiding eye contact with any of her companions. Kaiya made note of her action but did not draw attention to it. Her revelation had clearly unnerved the priestess.

She knows more than she's saying, Kaiya suspected. *But how is that possible?* Tashi had no magical talents, Kaiya was certain of it. This work was far too complicated

143

for a mere mortal. What Kaiya sensed in the rubble was a force unknown, one of tremendous strength. This was only the beginning of what it could do.

"There is great danger here," the sorceress said. "This avalanche was intentional, and the being who caused it is angry." To Raad, she asked, "Is there any plan in place for evacuation of the camps?"

He stammered over his words. "You'll have to speak to the foreman about that," he finally managed to say. Mines normally had an emergency evacuation plan for the miners, but for a camp this size full of women and children, he wasn't sure.

Looking back to the rocks, she said, "Maybe it won't come to that." There was still more to investigate, and she had yet to set foot inside the mine. Her vision showed her deep within the mountain as well as at its summit. "Tashi, do your people have any tales of magical beings who can cause rockslides or earthquakes?"

The priestess searched her memory but found nothing. "I have not heard such a tale," she replied. Glancing up toward the stars, she said, "The mountain is angry." Feeling smaller than ever before, she wanted to run into the night and hide herself. Eyes stared through her in the darkness—knowing eyes.

"Who angered it?" Galen asked.

Tashi looked away, her fingers trembling as she crossed her arms and squeezed them to her body. She couldn't tell them the truth. What would they do if they knew she had awakened this evil?

"If it gets angrier and the tremors get worse, then all dwarven lands might be in danger," Galen pointed out. "It could even reach the Vale." Nestled at the base of the Wrathful Mountains, the home of his people could be the next victim of rockslides, should this being decide to intensify its attacks.

"It's the miners' fault," Tashi spat, attempting to assuage her guilt. "They dug too deep and angered the mountain's heart." It was as good an explanation as any. With no magic of her own, how could she have summoned this evil? *I don't have that power*, she tried to convince herself. Though she wanted to believe that, she could not. She had seen the shadows and felt the dark presence. She was to blame.

"Now hold on there," Raad said, waving his finger. "You can't blame us for this."

"It isn't the mountain that's angry," Kaiya said. Her tone softened as she observed the priestess's discomfort. "It's something else, maybe something that's a part of the mountain itself." She couldn't be sure at this point. For one brief instant, she sensed the presence again, but it disappeared too quickly for any spell to take effect. Whatever it was, it was nearer now than before.

Rubbing her eyes, Kaiya tried to shake off her fatigue. "I guess it's time we get some sleep," she said, her mind too clouded to concentrate.

"Time for some ale," Raad replied. "You up for a trip to the tavern, Mr. Elf?"

"Sounds great," Galen replied.

"I'll come as well," Kaiya said, to the surprise of her male companions. "I'll never get to sleep without a drink."

"I thought you were against drinking," Raad said.

"I'm not against it," she corrected him. "What I'm against is drinking to the point of acting like an idiot, and I don't think one should drink at every opportunity. I just need enough to help me get a little sleep tonight." Without it, she feared her mind would never stop pondering over the magic in the rubble. She needed rest if she was going to function the next day.

"Come along then," the miner said cheerfully. "You too?" he asked Tashi.

"No," she replied. "I'd like to sleep now."

"Suit yourself," he said.

Her head held low, Tashi made her way down the path to the barracks Raad had pointed out. No one was inside, only silence. Choosing a bed near the wall, she climbed into it and drew the blankets up to her chin.

Since the death of her sister, she had not slept through a night. Her sleep was constantly disrupted by visions and strange noises, and the memory of death. A wave of pain traveled through her body, every muscle screaming with fatigue. She wished she'd thought to bring a sleep tonic. This strange place would offer little rest.

Nearly drifting off to sleep, the sound of an infant crying startled her back awake. Looking around the unfamiliar room, she reminded herself that her niece was not here. She was in the care of the doula, and she was safe. Tashi had to believe the girl was all right. But she had left her behind, so how could she be sure? The thought weighed heavily on her mind.

Closing her eyes, she lay back and steadied her breathing. Her sister's face gazed down at her from somewhere high above. Tashi could see the outline of a scowl on the young woman's lips. "Are you angry with me?" she whispered to the darkness.

The vision said nothing.

"You are ashamed of me for running away," Tashi said, sobbing. "I could not stay. It was too dangerous for our people."

Her sister remained silent.

"I might do some good here," Tashi said, hoping to convince her. "Maybe this sorceress can find a way to save our children and ensure our future."

Annin's visage faded away, leaving Tashi alone in the dark. "Sister!" she cried, her arms reaching out. No one was there to take them. Heartbroken, she buried her face in her pillow and wept.

* * * * *

A hush fell over the tavern patrons as the unusual guests entered. Two dwarves followed by an elf proceeded to the bar, their footsteps the only sound to be heard. No one in the room, save Kaiya and Raad, had ever laid eyes on an elf. Not a single man here had traveled beyond the mountains.

A dwarf with a frizzy red beard stepped forward, tilting his head to look Galen in the eye. Like every other dwarf in the room, he stood no taller than the elf's waist. "Where'd you come from?" he asked. His words were followed by a loud hiccup.

"The valley below the mountains," Galen replied, unoffended.

The man peered inside his mug. "Can you drink this stuff? You look awful delicate."

Galen couldn't help but laugh. "Oh yes, I can drink it. I've lived among dwarves for the past few years."

"You don't say," the dwarf replied, ale spilling down his beard. "Well, you're all right then," he announced, lifting his mug.

The noise level rose, the miners returning to their revelry.

Slapping a coin on the counter, the red-bearded dwarf said, "An ale for my friend here, and a refill for me."

The bartender obeyed. Nodding his thanks, Galen grasped the mug and downed half of its contents. The dwarf grinned and did the same.

Raad ordered a drink as well. "I'll pay for the lady's too," he told the bartender.

"Won't your wife be upset?" the dwarf jibed as he filled the mugs.

"She don't know I'm back yet," Raad replied with a smirk. "Best get a few drinks down me or she'll be hollerin' for me to get home and get some chores done."

"Thanks, Raad," Kaiya said, taking her drink from the dwarf behind the bar. Plopping herself on a low stool, she pressed the mug to her lips. With a large gulp, she took her first taste of the local ale. Rubbing her tongue against the roof of her mouth, she attempted to rid herself of the bitter flavor. *Raad was right,* she thought. *This isn't as good as down south.* The second sip wasn't as bad, and by the third, her tongue was accustomed to the flavor.

His cheeks reddening from ale, Galen burst into song, surprising the dwarves gathered around him. Kaiya had to cover her mouth to avoid spraying ale all over Raad, who was grinning from ear to ear as he listened in.

In a slurred tenor, the elf sang out.

"Once I met a dwarven girl,
her eyes like crystals shone.
She took me home and stripped me bare,
And skinned me to the bone!"

A raucous laughter filled the room, mugs slamming against the table to signal the miners' approval. Dwarves loved a good drinking song, the bawdier the better. Others took up the song, adding more to the story.

Kaiya enjoyed the moment of levity, especially seeing the joy it brought to Galen. He spent so much time studying the runes and reading that he rarely engaged in social activities. Proving he could be the life of the party, he made himself at home here among the miners, keeping time with his mug as the other men sang.

For a short time, Kaiya forgot about the evil presence. There was no talk of impending dangers or dark magic. In this moment, she was simply Kaiya, a dwarf girl from a farming village, enjoying a drink among friends.

Chapter 11

Pounding a fist heavily on the bunkhouse door, Raad's head throbbed. The noise echoed between his ears, amplified by the prior night's drink. He needed a pot of coffee, and quick. With any luck, he wouldn't have to make any more noise to wake those sleeping inside. Shoving open the door, he stepped inside.

Kaiya sat up, ready to start her day. Unlike the men, she had consumed only two drinks, and her mind was functioning perfectly. Stretching her arms, she nodded at Raad, whose eyes were reddened, his hair disheveled. A smile crept over her face as she wondered what his wife had said when he returned home in the wee hours of the morning.

The jest died on her lips as she glanced over at Tashi, who sat on the edge of her bed, staring at the back wall. Her head propped on one arm, and her shoulders slumped, the priestess appeared completely defeated. Throwing off her blanket, the sorceress swung her legs over the side of the bed and pulled on her shoes. Taking two steps toward Tashi, she paused at the sound of Raad's voice.

"Foreman's expecting you," he announced.

Glancing back at Tashi, she sighed. It would have to wait for another time. Whatever troubled the priestess, it was less important than figuring out what was causing the tremors. The foreman had information Kaiya desperately needed, at least she hoped he did. At the very least, he could give her permission to enter the mines to seek out the magic she sensed, and save her the need to break in.

Struggling out of his too-short bed, Galen found his way to Kaiya's side. "You want me to come along?" he asked, his mannerisms surprisingly normal considering the volume of drink he had guzzled.

"I think you best wait," Raad replied. "He'll want to meet an elf, for sure, but not right this moment. He asked for Kaiya alone."

"That'll give me time to explore the city," Galen said, unfazed. "You want to come along, Tashi?"

The priestess slowly rose from her bed and made her way toward the others. Her eyes focused on the narrow window, her mind a million miles away.

"You'll be headed back home, won't you?" Raad asked. "Some of the miners up here might think worse of your kind than I did. I'd hate to see any of them misunderstand."

"I don't fear them," she shot back, her voice full of venom.

"Now, don't start that," Raad replied. "I'll introduce all of you to Foreman Daro, then he and Kaiya can head off to the mine. I'll show you other two around the camp."

"Sounds like a plan," Galen replied. Glancing at Tashi, he saw no sign of change in her dour mood. He'd have to find some way to cheer her.

The morning sun barely peeked over the horizon, its soft-pink light illuminating the sky. Raad led the visitors westward, his every step labored. It was too early for this, and he would have much preferred to sleep in. But the foreman wouldn't wait. The bonus he'd paid Raad to fetch the sorceress was enough to keep the miner moving despite his lack of energy.

Straight ahead, a series of carts waited to ferry the miners to their work higher in the mountains. The steep terrain near the mine made habitation impossible, so a fifteen-minute ride was necessary to move the men to and from their worksite. Sturdy bighorn sheep, tamed by the skill of the dwarves, were well-suited to the task of pulling the carts over rough terrain.

Kaiya found the crowd surprisingly quiet as they awaited their turn on the carts. No other explanation came to her mind, save the early hour. Miners were hard workers, but few among them were morning people, regardless of their assigned shift. Rising early was the duty of farmers, like Kaiya's own father. It was likely due to him that she could fully appreciate the beauty of a sunrise.

By the time the visitors reached the miners, most of them had been loaded into their carts. Their wooden wheels crunching along the gravel path, they disappeared inside the morning mist. Raad signaled with a wave, drawing a single dwarf's attention.

Foreman Daro came forward with hurried steps, relieved to see that Raad had returned. A black-and-silver beard braided into a single row, along with a smoothly shaved head, gave the man a look of authority. His deep-brown eyes showed great concern, lines of worry creasing his brow.

"Raad," he said, nodding at the miner.

"Foreman Daro," Raad began, "this is Kaiya, the sorceress." Gesturing with his thumb, he said, "These are her friends, Galen and Tashi."

Daro's eyes darted between the visitors, unsure which to acknowledge first. It was Kaiya he had requested, but her friends were a sight to be seen. Extending a hand to Kaiya, he gripped hers firmly. "I'm glad you've come," he said. "We need your help. Are your friends here to help as well?"

"Tashi led us here through a path in the mountains," Kaiya replied. "Galen is an apprentice rune carver. He's come to consider the magical possibilities of Dwarf's Heart."

Daro's eyes danced with astonishment. "I'm delighted to meet you," he said, reaching for Galen's hand. A lifetime of fascination with creatures of magic, he felt nearly overwhelmed by the presence of a

Westerling Elf. Forcing himself not to stare, he turned his attention to Tashi. With a nod, he said, "I thank you for helping our visitors reach us safely."

Crossing her arms, the priestess did not reply.

"The Ulihi have a camp about day from here," Raad said, filling the awkward moment.

"We know about it," Daro admitted. "We know about the path too, but we stay clear of it." The mining company that employed Daro had been thorough in surveying the land. For the most part, they had done their best to avoid disturbing the Ulihi in their current encampment.

"This mine is built on our hunting grounds," Tashi finally said.

"I can't help that," Daro said. "This is where the Dwarf's Heart is, so this is where we had to build. We're aware of your tribe, and we won't bother you if you don't bother us."

Heat rose in Tashi's face. "You've already bothered us!" she shouted. "Why do your kind insist they own this land? No one can own it. The mountain is its own master."

"I don't doubt that, Miss Tashi," the foreman replied. "But we've claimed it for the time being. If you want to represent your people at the next company meeting, I'll see that your voice is heard."

Blinking in surprise, Tashi didn't know how to reply. Kaiya smiled, her heart full as she tried to catch Tashi's eye. When she finally did, she nodded, encouraging her companion to speak.

"I would like that," Tashi stammered. "Thank you."

Daro waved the words away. "It's the least I can do," he said. Focusing his attention to Kaiya, he asked, "Are you ready to inspect the mine?"

Finding herself suddenly nervous, she took in a deep breath and said, "I am."

"Will you be joining us?" he asked Galen.

"I—" Galen started to say.

"If I may," Kaiya cut in. "It would be easier for me if Galen stayed behind. His elven magic will be a distraction as I search for the source of power I've felt in this area."

"I understand," Daro replied. "I've heard magic radiates from an elf's hair." He took a moment to scan the length of Galen's hair, wondering what mysteries hid themselves within it.

"I'll look after these two for you," Raad said. Hopefully another trip to the tavern would make its way onto the agenda. With his arm feeling better, the following day would mark his return to the mines, which meant today shouldn't go to waste.

"Shall we?" Daro asked, gesturing his hand to the remaining cart.

Accepting his hand, Kaiya stepped onto the cart, the bighorns pawing with impatience as she found her seat. Daro signaled the driver to head out, and the team lunged forward, eager to be underway.

"It's the deepest mine that any dwarf's ever dug," Daro said. "We'll be there in a few minutes."

"Tell me why you needed a sorceress," Kaiya replied. It was time for some answers.

Shifting in his seat, the foreman said, "You know about the avalanches. We've had a lot of men hurt, and the mining company is losing money."

"An avalanche or two is to be expected," Kaiya stated.

"Naturally," Daro replied. "But something isn't right in there. I'm no mage, but I've had an interest in magical enchantments since I was young. It's a feeling

I get down in those tunnels." Looking away, he added, "I suppose it sounds silly."

"Not at all," the sorceress replied. "Even those without magic can sometimes sense its presence."

The foreman swiveled his head back toward her. "You mean that?"

"I do," she said. "There is magic here. I can feel it too."

A sigh of relief escaped the dwarf's lips. "That already makes me feel better. I was afraid I might be overreacting."

"I don't think you'll feel better for long," she replied. "What I sense is malice, an evil heart bent on destruction. Even now, it echoes in my chest." As they moved closer to the mine, Kaiya's fingers shook, a tingling sensation buzzing through them. Something was testing her, a tug at her magical stores confirmed it. Each breath came faster as she forced herself to remain seated, fighting the instinct to run toward the mine. Or was it the urge to flee? Grinding her teeth, she did her best to steady her mind.

"Are my men safe in there?" Daro asked, leaning toward her.

"I don't know," she replied honestly. "I have to go down there to find out."

Stopping near the mine entrance, the driver set the brake and waited for his passenger to disembark. Daro assisted Kaiya as she stepped down before sending the driver away. Kaiya paused outside the mine, her eyes staring intently into the darkness. The color drained from her face.

"You all right?" Daro asked, laying a hand on her shoulder. Her pale visage unnerved him, her silence alarming.

Kaiya gave no answer, her hand reaching for a lantern as she stepped inside the mine. Daro followed closely behind, grabbing a lantern of his own. Upon entry, the path descended. Kaiya immediately made note of the lack of fresh air. The ventilation system required for such a massive pit would have to be extensive, but it provided no wind. Miners were not able to stay down as long as usual, forcing the work to be done in four shifts rather than the standard three.

Stillness cut through Kaiya, panic running along her spine. With much effort, she forced herself to remain calm. Here, more than any other place, she was vulnerable.

Dim lanterns lined the walls, a system of movable platforms descending to and from the depths. Stepping onto the platform, she waited for Daro to pull the lever.

"Down we go," he said.

They sank into the darkness, the music of mining picks serenading them along the way. Dots of green light illuminated the walls, a gift of the glowworms that inhabited the mines. Without these creatures, the miners digging at the lowest depths would be forced to work in complete darkness, the lanterns barely able to draw enough oxygen to remain lit. The flame in Kaiya's hand flickered, reducing itself to the size of a pea. More an item of comfort than of practicality, the lanterns were nearly useless.

A buzzing entered Kaiya's muscles, radiating throughout her body as they arrived at the first plateau. Stepping off the platform, Kaiya stumbled, righting herself before Daro could notice. To her relief, a system of mirrors stood at various angles, catching light from above and projecting it along the pathway to the lifts. Taking courage from the light, she drove the buzzing away without the use of magic.

"How many levels are there?" she asked, peering over the ledge.

"Three," Daro replied. "There aren't any workers at the bottom. I assume that's where you want to go?"

"Yes," she replied, though she wanted to say no. A low voice called from the depths, urging her ever downward. Though she'd come here to confront it, she wasn't sure she wanted to. The stillness raged around her, and should she require the use of her magic, her stores could quickly become depleted. Lacking the element required for replenishment put her at great risk.

Her eyes finally adjusted to the darkness, Kaiya followed Daro as he led the way down to the second plateau and made his way across the expansive deep. The third platform, the one that led down to the deepest level, lay just ahead.

"I'll go alone from here," she announced as they reached the platform.

"You sure?" Daro asked. "The light barely reaches down there, and it's easy to get lost."

"I need complete concentration," she replied. "I'm afraid your presence could distract me." Even the quietest dwarves were typically noisy, and she would need complete silence. "Can you order your men to stop hammering until I return?"

"Aye," he replied. "I'll do that and come right back to this spot. You can shout when you're ready for me to bring you back up."

The sorceress agreed out of politeness. She was quite capable of pulling herself back up, her arms not lacking for strength. But Daro was unused to women inside his mine, so he treated her with as great a care as he would any lady.

Steadying herself on the platform, she waited patiently as Daro lowered her into the darkness. The light faded to a dull gray, the pinpoint lights of the glowworms outshining that which was brought down by the mirrors. Here the world was entirely still, her lungs working overtime to find fresh air. Once again the buzzing returned, traveling up her spine and settling in the back of her head. Her ears puffed, and she swallowed hard to drive the feeling away.

Setting aside her now-useless lantern, she tuned her ears to the stillness. A voice called out, a low rumbling tone. More curiosity than anger, whoever it was wanted to know her better.

Where are you? she projected with her mind.

There was no change to the voice. It held the same steady tone, beckoning her toward it. Keeping one hand against the wall, she kept herself in check. With a ceiling that stretched up to eternity, and the darkness surrounding her, it would be all too easy to lose her bearings.

Twisting along the wide path, she followed the rumbling sound. Above her all fell silent, no hammers echoing throughout the mine. The pounding of her heart replaced the hammers, but she found her courage and steadied her breathing, forcing her legs to keep moving.

Rounding a bend, the path became unsteady, small rocks sliding beneath her feet. The way narrowed into a single passageway, wide enough for only two men at a time. Still moving forward, the rumbling grew louder, but a wall blocked her way. Taking in what she could make out in the black, she believed this to be the end of the mine. A pile of rubble had been placed to one side, awaiting its transport outside. The tunnel was too small for a large team of miners, meaning it must still be under excavation.

Placing her hand flat against the uneven floor, she searched for the owner of the voice. Her mind penetrated the rock, scanning the undiscovered depths. Passing deposits of iron and painite, she pressed on, searching for her quarry.

There, in the depths, she saw it, a vision through the stone. Massive, far taller than an elf, far stouter than a dwarf. It lifted its mighty head, its mouth open wide to reveal the fire within. A roar of anger shook the walls, debris raining down upon her. Still she held her concentration, her mind examining every feature of this monster. Magic radiated from it, a long-dormant master of earth, fed by the rock surrounding it.

Trapped.

Who had bound this creature to this place? Only the Ancients had such power. Kaiya scanned her memory for any old tales that might explain what he was. A spark of realization hit her. The mountain itself had entombed this colossus. How long had it been there?

A dizziness nearly knocked her off her feet. This creature was far out of her league. She could not face such ancient magic. She was too young, too inexperienced. What was forty years in the lifetime of a mountain? Her inadequacies overwhelming, she pulled her mind away from the depths.

Awake.

One last word echoed in her ears. What had lain dormant for millennia was about to rise. Reeling from this discovery, she struggled for a breath. Stumbling in the darkness, her thoughts focused only on retreat. But her feet would not obey, and she found herself rooted in place. Something drew near.

Chapter 12

With a sickening snap, the wall before the sorceress broke open, and a bipedal creature of stone emerged. Its head reared back, and its mouth gaped open to let out a single raspy cry. Kaiya jumped backward, stumbled in the darkness, and landed hard on her side.

The creature closed in, its heavy footfalls ringing in her ears. Its purpose to destroy, it would not stop until the dwarf lay crushed beneath its weight. Her sense of direction lost to the darkness, Kaiya found her back against a wall. It was now or never.

Reaching deep into her magical stores, she summoned an energy blast to knock her pursuer off-course. With one hand she sent the blast hurling toward its midsection, with the other she summoned a light. As the cavern illuminated, she glimpsed the creature whirring to the side, trying to stay balanced despite the burst of energy nearly knocking it over. Finding an opening, Kaiya dashed for it, putting some distance between herself and the beast.

Deafening vibrations from the creature's stride assaulted her ears, her head pounding as she readied herself for another attack. The light at her fingertips gave her a clear view of her pursuer, its misshapen body haphazardly thrown together. Its limbs uneven, its gait unsteady, Kaiya's confidence rose. It reared its head once more, its bellowing cry rattling through her body.

Planting her feet firmly against the floor, Kaiya refused to be intimidated. She would fight, not flee. Before dousing her light to preserve magic, she made note of the lowered section of ceiling in the unfinished tunnel. A triangular chunk of rock dangled precariously, waiting for her to take advantage.

Sensing the danger it was in, the creature charged toward her, chunks of rock splitting off of its body. Kaiya held fast, ignoring the rocks that pelted her. With a flash of silver in her eyes, she summoned enough heat to saw through the base of the triangular stone. Before she could finish, the creature closed in, its rocky arms swinging wildly. Pirouetting to the left, she narrowly avoided a collision between her head and the creature's arm, but now she was cornered.

Hoping the heat spell had been enough, she blasted energy at the triangular rock. Careening to the floor, it landed with a thunderous crash. Unfazed by the sound, the creature moved forward, closing in on the trapped dwarf, a hint of laughter in its voice. Pulling back its arm, it prepared for the killing blow.

Her lungs begging for air, Kaiya knew she didn't have long. Without a clear view of the sky, she could not summon the lightning as she had with the last beast. Alone in the darkness, she would have to throw everything she had left at the beast if she hoped to escape.

Calling on the remainder of her magical stores, she tapped into the cavern's remaining air. Its elemental power radiating from her fingertips, she pushed with all her strength, forcing its energy into the triangular rock. Spinning through the air, the rock sailed toward the beast, smashing into its midsection and splitting it in two. With the last of her strength, she sent the stone upward, shattering it against the ceiling, rubble raining down on the creature. Buried beneath the debris, the beast lay still.

Charging past the destruction, Kaiya raced for the platform. Dizzy and out of breath, she fought her way through the stillness. As she reached for the rope to pull herself up, she realized her arms had gone numb. A lump rose in her throat, preventing her from crying out for help.

Nearly frantic, she stood upon the platform for what felt like an eternity. To her relief, the creaking of the pulley alerted her that someone was headed down. Dropping to her knees, she glimpsed Daro, accompanied by three miners, descending to her level.

The foreman scooped her up as if she weighed nothing and signaled one of the others to raise the platform. "We have to get her out of here," he said.

Nearly dragging her outside the mine, Daro helped her to a seat and fanned the air in front of her face.

"I'm all right," she managed to squeak out. Though exhausted, the sudden exposure to her element was quickly replenishing her magic. Soon she would feel rested and recharged.

"We heard the racket down there," Daro said, his voice quiet. "Was it one of those rock beasts?"

Stunned, Kaiya stared at the foreman. "How did you know?" she asked.

"One showed up a week or so ago," he replied. "It took more than twenty men to stop it. That's why I sent for you."

"You might have told me," she said, annoyed.

"I swore Raad to secrecy," he replied, shaking his head and looking at the ground. "I wasn't sure how you'd react to that sort of thing, and I didn't want to risk your not coming. I'm sorry."

"Is there anything else you'd like to tell me?" she asked.

"You know everything I do," he replied. "Do you think we woke up something down there?"

"Something has awakened, but I'm not sure mining is the cause." Feeling the soothing touch of the wind upon her face, she finally had the energy to stand. "What became of the rock beast the miners fought?"

"We tossed it aside with the rubble from the avalanche," he replied.

That explained the magic Kaiya had sensed in the debris. Straining her ears to the breeze, she listened for its counsel. "It's time for this being to wake," she said as if in a trance. "No matter how much noise the dwarves made, it wouldn't have awoken unless it was ready."

Daro stared at her in awe.

Her normal demeanor returning, Kaiya warned, "I wouldn't dig any deeper than you already have. Unless you want to run into it face to face."

"What will this thing do when it finally makes its way to the surface?" he asked.

"It is bent on destruction," she replied. "I have to stop it before it manages to free itself."

"Whatever you need from me, it's yours," the foreman pledged. To safeguard the lives of his crew and their families, he would spare no expense. "I knew it was a good idea to bring you here," he added. Her willingness to stand against this being was admirable. Daro could tell she would fight to the end. After all, she'd singlehandedly taken down a rock beast. In his eyes, she was more than a sorceress—she was a hero.

* * * * *

It was a quiet ride back to the camp, the wheels in Kaiya's mind grinding. When the cart came to a halt, she stepped out without so much as glancing at the driver. Her eyes instead scanned the area for her companions. A slender figure, whose tribal manner of dress made her easy to single out, paced nervously back and forth. Not far from her stood Galen, and next to him Raad.

Waving at the sight of his friend, Galen called out to her. "Back so soon?" he asked, the smile fading from his lips as she approached. Her demeanor was far too severe for humor.

"You're wounded!" Tashi shouted as she came to Kaiya's side. Ignoring all rules of personal space, she touched her fingers to the sorceress's face. "How could these foul men allow you to come to harm?" she spat.

"It's just a few scrapes and bruises," Kaiya assured her. "The air will soon heal them." Gently she took Tashi's hands in hers and moved them from her face. Squeezing them tightly, she said, "I do appreciate your concern."

Released from the sorceress's grip, Tashi's arms dangled at her side, her fingers fidgeting against her palms. Before her eyes, Kaiya's wounds did indeed repair themselves. The purplish bruises gave way to fresh skin, the cuts sealing themselves until barely visible. "Amazing," she whispered.

"Did you find anything?" Raad asked.

"At the lowest level of the mines, I had a vision," Kaiya began. "A massive creature crafted of stone lives deep within the heart of the mountain. It is angry, all its thoughts bent on destruction."

"What else did you see?" Galen asked, knowing she was holding back.

"When it opened its mouth, I saw fire," she said. "I made out only two words: trapped and awake."

"Who spoke the words?" the elf asked.

Kaiya thought a moment. "When I was in the mine, I was certain it was the creature's voice. Now I'm not so certain. But who else could it have been?"

The trio exchanged glances, but none had an answer to her question.

"What manner of beast lives inside a mountain?" Tashi asked, her voice shaking. Silently she hoped there was some explanation other than the one she held in her heart.

"It could only be an Ancient," Kaiya answered.

"No," Galen replied. "It isn't an Ancient."

"What do you mean?" she asked, confused.

"The Ancients were creators," Galen explained. "What you saw in your vision is a Gawr. It is a being of destruction."

"But how else could it be old enough to live at the heart of the mountain?" Kaiya asked. "It couldn't have dug itself that deep—even the dwarves don't have such skill. It must have been there when the mountain was created."

"Whoever your Ancients are, they did not create the mountain," Tashi said, drawing everyone's attention. "The mountain always was, and always will be."

"Tashi's right," Galen said with a knowing smile. "The mountain was here when the Ancients first came. The Gawr was already here as well. They could neither create nor destroy it. It is, as you said, a part of the mountain."

"How do you know all this?" Tashi asked. "Do your people pass down tales as mine do?"

"We do," Galen replied, "but I read about the Gawr in an old book."

177

"Ink on parchment told you of this?" she asked, her eyes full of wonder.

"They did," he replied.

"I would like to learn this skill you possess," she stated.

"I'd be honored to teach you," he responded.

"Are you telling me that the Gawr wants to destroy everything some ancient elves created?" Raad asked.

"More than that," he replied. "It wants to destroy the world itself. All life, all beings. By destroying the world's foundation, it could end everything at once."

After a moment's thought, Kaiya asked, "Did the Ancients know of the Gawr?"

"Yes," he answered. "They were able to control it."

"Are you going to tell me how?" the sorceress asked, losing patience. "Or are you going to stand here chatting until the world splits apart?"

"The words you heard already told you what to do," he replied, his tone calm. "The Gawr has awakened, and only powerful magic can lull it back to sleep, essentially trapping it in its own domain."

Kaiya looked up toward the mountain's summit. "I lack the power of the Ancients," she admitted. "If I had an army of elementals, maybe…"

"Then all is lost," Tashi said, tears splashing on her face. "I have doomed my people, and all the world."

"This isn't your fault," Galen said, wrinkling his brow.

"Kaiya, I must speak with you." Tashi said. "In private."

Though her mind whirled as she attempted to process Galen's information, Kaiya nodded and stepped away with Tashi at her side. The pair headed away from the camp, finding their way to a series of boulders.

"This is far enough," Kaiya announced, taking a seat and motioning for Tashi to do likewise.

But Tashi could not sit. She paced, unable to make eye contact with Kaiya. "I…" she stammered, not knowing where to begin.

"You said you doomed your people," Kaiya said. "Tell me why you think that."

"I brought this evil upon us," she replied, her throat aching from the words. "I did it to save my sister." She sobbed, wiping her tears with the back of her hand.

"I don't understand," Kaiya replied. She was not without sympathy, her heart yearning to help the troubled woman. But she did not understand the problem, and there was a much bigger issue to tend to. "Tell me everything, and do it quickly," she demanded.

"The rock beast that attacked my village," the priestess began. "It came because of me. I woke its master. I thought my people were safe without me in the village." Her words trailed off.

"You left because the rock beast came for you?" Kaiya asked, trying to understand.

"I prayed to the dead god," Tashi replied, falling to her knees before the sorceress. "I performed the ancient ritual and sealed it with blood. Annin was dying. I would have done anything to save her."

"The dead god?" Kaiya shook her head. "Is that what the Gawr is to your people?"

"A giant of stone, banished to the heart of the world by the other gods. For his misdeeds he was punished. They never intended for him to wake, but I summoned him. I knew the cost."

Kaiya looked upon the woman with pity. Her remorse was genuine, her regret deeper than any the sorceress could imagine.

"You must understand," Tashi said, choking on her tears. "The bond between sisters is more powerful than any other. Friends and lovers come and go, but your sister is yours always. She shares your pain, your joy, your reason for being. To lose a sister is to lose one's heart."

Having never had a sister, Kaiya didn't know how Tashi felt. She loved her brothers, but they were much older than her. She had grown up almost like an only child, the wind her closest friend. An outcast among her kind, her parents had showered her with all the love she needed. Not once had she desired the existence of a sister. Only now did she wonder what it might have been like, and how far she might have gone to help her. *Could I trade the world for my sister?* she wondered. It was an impossible question to answer.

"It's too late to change the past," Kaiya finally said. "Now we must find a way to preserve the future." *Before there is no future to preserve,* she silently added.

"I risked my eternal soul by waking this god," Tashi said. "I will accept its wrath upon myself in the hope that it will spare the world. I have no magic to offer you, but I beg you to let me help make this right."

"I don't know if I have the power either," Kaiya admitted.

"Only the gods have true power," Tashi replied, but then corrected herself. "Had power, or maybe they never did. Either way, they will not answer my prayers."

"I've never put much store in gods," the sorceress replied. "But I promise you this: I will fight this beast with every ounce of strength in my body, and every drop of magic the wind can produce."

Chapter 13

Alone, Kaiya trekked nearly a mile through the rough terrain, searching for a suitable location. All must be silent if she was to meditate properly. No hammers ringing, no children's voices. This was far too important an issue for her to misunderstand.

Choosing a suitable spot in the presence of an evergreen, Kaiya took a seat on the soft earth that luckily was clear of snow. Crossing her legs, she found them surprisingly sore. The wind had healed her cuts and bruises, but the effects of her depletion still lingered. Taking a few deep breaths, she attempted to comfort and calm herself.

Turning her face skyward, she pondered the blue of the heavens. Soft, white clouds strolled lazily by, carried on a wind so pure, she desired to travel alongside them. Focusing only on the blue, she pushed away thoughts of the evil that threatened to rise, as well as her own self-doubt.

The wind was ancient, born before time itself. It had witnessed the rise and fall of civilizations, the formation of all Nōl'Deron. Along with fire, water, and earth, it had assisted the Ancients in shaping this world. It knew the Gawr from its inception. If it did not know a way to stop this creature, then all would be lost.

Continuing her deep breaths, she trained herself to inhale quickly while drawing out her exhalation. A calm settled over her mind, only one thought brimming to the surface.

Show me the way.

Obliging its mistress, the wind obeyed, a vision descending into the sorceress's mind. Images so clear, she felt as if she had seen them with her own eyes played out before her, time moving backward until she could barely recognize the landscape.

A world of rock, fire at its center, took shape as she bore witness. No life-forms were present, not even the smallest hint of green, but still she sensed a presence.

There was a life here, the same one she had felt in her earlier vision, the one that she had felt in the mines.

A sky filled with stars, the occasional streak of fire darting across the blackness filled the sorceress with wonder. Varied colors of swirling mists painted the night sky, colors she had never seen before. Feeling that she'd stepped onto another world, she could do no more than watch in awe.

A blinding flash of light changed the scene before her. In place of the Wrathful Mountains stood a volcano, smoke and flame belching from its center. Feeling herself perspire beneath the oppressive heat, Kaiya fought against her discomfort. In the distance, she spotted what must have been the ocean, steam rising from its surface. The water level was surprisingly high, but this was history far beyond what was written. Only the Ancients could know what the world was like at this point.

Slowly she adjusted to the heat, her mind clearing enough to reach out. There, in the fiery center of the volcano, lived the Gawr. Here it seemed content, almost complacent. There was no anger, but there was hatred. Without warning, the ground shook beneath her feet, the volcano spewing ash. A violent earthquake ravaged the hillside, deep crags ripping across the landscape. Seconds later, all was covered in dust. Instinctively she coughed and held up her arm to shield her eyes.

Another burst of light turned the page on her vision, transporting her to a snow-capped mountain. The exact opposite of the land she'd just witnessed, this place was extremely cold. A thick coat of ice entombed all she could see, a chilled wind stinging her face. Still the Gawr made itself known. A low rumbling gave way to great cracks in the ice, massive chunks falling away to form glaciers of blue and white. Her breath caught in her chest as she witnessed the rise of the mountain, the earth beneath it reaching ever higher, thrusting the summit toward the sky.

Before the sight could overwhelm her, a silver light flared, bringing yet another change. This time people stood before her, the wind whispering one word: Ancients. Tall and slender, with a strong resemblance to Galen's people, stood four figures radiating immense power. It was now obvious why the Westerling Elves referred to themselves as the First Ones. There could be no doubt they had descended from the Ancients, the first to be created by their glorious hands. A yearning settled into her heart as she desired to know these people better.

I wish to speak with them, she projected on the wind.

It isn't possible, came the reply.

Kaiya grunted in frustration. Even the wind had its limits. It could not transport her through time. This was only a vision; the Ancients weren't really standing before her. A bitter disappointment tasted on her tongue, tears welling in her eyes. These people had the answer she sought, but how would she coax it from them if she couldn't speak to them?

Patience, the wind reminded her.

Watching the scene play out, Kaiya felt a renewed sense of peace. Yes, the Gawr was still present, but it was somewhere in the background, all but forgotten. One of the Ancients, a male with white hair, gazed at the ground. As she pondered what he might be doing, she caught the scent of a soft rainfall. To her surprise, the Ancients took no shelter, but she had to resist the instinct for herself. Though she was quite dry, it still hadn't fully registered that she was only a witness to the scene, not a part of it.

The white-haired Ancient continued to stare at the ground, no words escaping his lips. With thought alone, he brought forth green sprouts, which shot up to his own height within seconds. Taking the form of evergreens, proud and strong, they ascended toward the heavens, their needled arms reaching out in all directions. Amazed, she wondered if any of these trees still existed. Surely time could not undo such wonders.

A woman with raven hair that tumbled to her ankles stood in the background, her arms waving delicately, mimicking the flight of a bird. Through her motion, streams began to form. A mere trickle at first, they expanded, gliding down the mountainside before diving over the edges. Pristine waterfalls gave life to the rivers below, their lush waters flowing toward eternity.

The sight was too much for the sorceress, and she wept but did not avert her gaze. Such beauty was not meant for her eyes, but the wind had granted her this gift. The daughter of a farmer, she had always loved and respected the land. But seeing its creation, and feeling the love in the hearts of its creators, was an experience like no other.

Gently the wind dried her tears, its unseen hands wrapping her in their warmth. She steadied herself, knowing what was to come. There was still more to see, and this scene had reached its end. A burst of white light moved her forward in time, the world transforming to a state of chaos.

A wave of shock traveled through her as her mind registered the horrific scene. How could such beauty come to complete destruction? What power could have done this? Immediately the presence of the Gawr announced itself. Its voice shouting, fire spewing from its open mouth. An indescribably joy emanated from the vile creature as it reveled in the carnage.

Kaiya attempted to close her eyes, hoping to block out the scene in front of her, but the wind would not allow it. She must witness things as it had seen them if she was to understand. The truth could not be denied.

Flames spread over the once-green forests, the massive trees brought to life by the Ancients fell victim to the Gawr, consumed in its raging fire. Furred creatures darted from their hiding places, desperately trying to outrun the inferno. She could not count the number that did not make it. Birds fled above her, forced from their nests by the rising smoke, their chicks left unprotected and helpless. Her mouth went dry, the taste of ash assaulting her tongue.

Wrapping her arms around herself, Kaiya tried to force the image to change. This was more than she could bear, her heart breaking, the pain traveling throughout every vein. And still the Gawr projected its immense delight. A cry of pure ecstasy issued from its lungs.

Bracing herself against the shuddering of the ground, Kaiya barely managed to stay upright. The shaking was more intense than before, rocks falling loose and tumbling in every direction. Great clouds of gray dust swirled on the wind, clouding her vision. With her hand held above her eyes, she strained to see what appeared before her.

Misshapen forms emerged from the rubble, some on two legs, some on four or more. Her heart leapt to her throat as her mind raced to devise a plan of action.

Far too many beasts appeared, more than she could handle alone. None of them took notice of the sorceress. *I'm not really here,* she reminded herself. They passed by her, no trace of malice in them at all. There was nothing left for them to destroy.

The dust began to clear, but not before tickling the delicate hairs inside Kaiya's nostrils. Wiggling her nose, she expected to sneeze but didn't. Instead the dust settled, and all became still. Unnerved, Kaiya wondered why the scene had not changed.

Again the rumbling returned, this time accompanied by a sharper noise, as if the world were splitting into pieces. Chunks of the mountain plummeted down the cliffside, racing toward her. Rooted to the spot, her feet as heavy as lead, she could not move out of the way. Instinctively, she reached for her magic, attempting to reroute the boulders. Silver magic flew from her fingertips, but the rocks did not obey.

Holding her breath, she braced herself for impact. The boulder passed through her, causing her no harm. Doubling over with relief, she felt the wind in her hair. *You're not in any danger,* she scolded herself, redness creeping into her cheeks. *This is the wind's memory.* Apparently she still needed to convince herself. The scenes were all too real.

Floating on the wind's embrace, Kaiya welcomed the flash of light that put an end to the ghastly scene. Once again life teemed in the mountains, the Ancients standing before her. Two women and one man stood engrossed in conversation. The same white-haired man and raven-haired woman were accompanied by a second female. Her dark hair was cropped short, but her face was strikingly similar to the raven-haired Ancient. Kaiya decided the two had to be sisters.

"We must take action, Elnar," the short-haired woman insisted.

"The stone giant is too dangerous," Elnar, the white-haired man, replied.

"What say you, Tienna?" the short-haired woman asked.

"The only action we can take is to correct the destruction the Gawr has brought to this land." Tienna's voice was full of sorrow, her eyes averted to the ground.

"We'll have to do so every time he wakes," the short-haired woman replied. "That leaves little time for anything else. We must act!"

"We cannot change the Gawr's nature, Zarla," Tienna said, her voice full of regret. "It must do as its nature insists. It cannot change what it is."

"Unacceptable," Zarla replied.

"The Gawr is a jealous beast," Elnar said. "It wishes to create but has only the ability to destroy. That's why all of its attempts at creation take the form of misshapen monsters."

"And if it has its way, it will fill the world with those abominations," Zarla added.

Kaiya knew to which creatures the Ancients referred. The rock beasts were unnatural, crafted by the destroyer.

"As long as we allow it to exist, it will continue to unleash this horror," Zarla went on. With a wave of her hand, she drew their attention to the ruination all around. Trees stripped bare of green lay dying upon a field of rubble; no song of birds sounded from the skies. All life had been lost to the malice of the Gawr. "All we have created will perish in time. We must stop this."

"We cannot," Elnar replied. "It is not in our nature to destroy, even one such as the Gawr."

"I will not sit by while this happens again and again," Zarla warned, her visage darkening.

Tienna stepped forward, gently taking her sister's hand. "The Gawr must rest," she said, her voice a song upon the wind. "I shall sing him to sleep, but he will not remain that way. Others will have to maintain the spell, or the cycle of destruction and rebirth will continue."

Zarla nodded her agreement as did Elnar. The trio joined hands, Tienna turning her face to the heavens. Kaiya focused her full attention to the raven-haired Ancient, determined to commit her song to memory.

A lullaby found its way to the sorceress's ears—a strange, unintelligible song. Such language Kaiya had never heard, nor could she imagine herself being able to vocalize such sounds. Was this the language of the Ancients? Notes rose and fell, some of them too high for the dwarf to comprehend. Stifling a cry of frustration in her throat, she clenched her fists and turned to her magic, but she knew no spell that could capture a song.

Keep watching the wind whispered. Kaiya obeyed.

All fell silent as the song ended, the image of the Ancients fading into darkness. Tienna and Zarla appeared, and behind them stood several Ulihi. Kaiya could not hear what the Ancients said to them, but they appeared enraptured by their presence. A priestess in a beaded headdress stepped forward, taking Tienna by the hand, while Zarla drew lines on the ground with a silver beam of magic. Kneeling down together, the Ancients traced the three distinct symbols drawn into the dust, carefully explaining each to the priestess.

Kaiya strained her eyes to see the lines more clearly. They glistened in a multitude of hues before settling permanently to a deep shade of red. Magic shimmered upon the runes, the images burning themselves into Kaiya's memory. It was not the song she needed to remember, but the runes.

Before her eyes flashed a series of images: three distinct locations high in the mountains. Again and again, the images repeated themselves, the runes flashing before her upon a sea of red. "Dwarf's Heart," Kaiya whispered to the wind. Closing her eyes, she sucked air deep into her lungs. "Now I understand."

Chapter 14

Rubbing her eyes, Kaiya studied the scene before her. No more visions—she saw only the landscape as it had been when she sat down. Hope entered her heart, a feeling of peace she had not expected. The wind had revealed its full knowledge of the Gawr, and the method for besting it. Using the same technique the Ancients taught the Ulihi, Kaiya could set this right.

Taking one step forward, she stumbled, the earth beneath her giving way. Grasping at the edge of the sinkhole, she summoned the wind to lift her over the side. Rocks slid away beneath her fingers, but she did not lose her grip. The wind obeyed, lightening her load and allowing her to lift herself out.

A searing heat rose through her body, the red eyes of the Gawr upon her. It knew what the wind knew, and it would use any means to stop Kaiya. The wind tousled her violet locks as she projected with her mind, *I'm coming for you.* Swallowing her fear, she summoned the wind to shield her. The Gawr must not follow her steps. She would never make it up the mountainside if it did. Rock slides and tremors would make the journey impossible.

But how much power did the Gawr truly have? After all, it was not fully awake. The process to restrain it took time, and Kaiya hoped she would have enough. If it was beyond the Ancients to defeat this creature, it was surely beyond her. Only the power of the runes would send this monster to its rest.

Carefully making her way back to the village, Kaiya kept her focus on her feet. With the wind as her companion, she monitored the ground, looking for the first sign of an attack. The Gawr would not feel her footsteps, but it knew where she would go. There was no time to lose. She must act before it could.

The camp was bustling with activity, men and loaded wagons heading in all directions. She stopped a passing child to ask, "Have you seen the elf and the Ulihi woman?" It was all the description necessary.

"Sure have!" the boy replied. "They're over by the Dwarf's Heart cutters."

"And where is that exactly?" she asked.

"Head down this path," the boy said, pointing ahead. "Go to the end, and make a right. It's the third shop on your right." He beamed with pride, happy to be of help.

"Thanks," Kaiya said. She hurried along the road, dodging a cartload of linens and earning a few choice words from its driver. Paying him no heed, she continued following the boy's directions. To her delight, she could clearly see Tashi, seated on a low wooden stool.

The priestess stood at the dwarf's approach. "Did you learn anything?" she asked.

"I did," Kaiya replied. "Where is Galen?"

"Raad brought us here so the elf could work with the gem cutters," Tashi said. "He's in the workshop." Motioning for Kaiya to follow, she pulled open the door.

Several work stations awaited inside, manned by busy dwarves scrutinizing the gems before them. Each man held a magnifying glass, his face pressed close to the unrefined mineral.

"I guess this is where they prepare the Dwarf's Heart before sending it to the elves," Kaiya commented.

"Your elf friend says these red rocks hold magical powers," Tashi replied. "He was excited to come here."

"Why didn't you come inside with him?" Kaiya wondered.

"I prefer not to be confined with so many...people," she said.

"You mean dwarves?" the sorceress asked with a smile.

Tashi did not reply. She did not wish to offend Kaiya, whose company she found pleasant. But a room full of dwarf men, all obsessed with shiny trinkets, was not somewhere she wanted to be for long. Besides, she had no interest in the gemstones. Having no practical use, they were of no value to the Ulihi.

A loud gasp from Kaiya stopped Tashi in her tracks, her hand gripping tightly to her staff. "What is it?" she asked.

Clapping her hands over her mouth, Kaiya slowly approached one of the work stations. Behind the table, Galen gave a cheerful wave.

"Your hair," Kaiya said, her hands slowly sliding from her lips. "What? Who?" Her words tripped over her tongue and landed hard against the back of her teeth.

"I'm going for a new look," Galen replied, running his fingers through his dark hair. What had once cascaded down his back, landing at his waist, was now cropped close to his scalp. "Do you like it?"

Still stuttering, she replied, "It's certainly different."

"That's just the look I was going for," he replied cheerfully. "Come and see what else I've done."

Still staring at his hair, she approached the work table and observed his hands. He clutched a small bit of stone in one hand, the other covered in dirt from his work. When he held the item up for her to observe, her mouth dropped open. Inlaid within the stone was a rune, fashioned in the same blood red color she had seen in her vision. Magic gleamed on the rune's surface.

"It's the symbol for air," he said, passing her the stone. "I made it for you."

The rune stone tingled in her hand, its magic warming her fingers. At a loss for words, she held the stone toward the light to observe it better.

"I made it from one of the spent stones of the rock beast," Galen explained. "The inlay is Dwarf's Heart." Dusting his hands and wiping them on his pants, he added, "Its magic will give you strength, should you ever go where the wind can't watch over you."

Kaiya felt a lump rise in her throat. Not only had a great deal of effort gone into this gift, a great deal of coin had too. Dwarf's Heart was not easily purchased by any but the wealthiest of nobles. Immediately, she knew the real reason he had cut his hair. He traded it to Daro, who believed in its magical properties. It was the only way Galen could afford the painite. "Thank you," she managed to say, clutching the gift in her hand.

"There's nothing I wouldn't do for you," the elf said.

Her eyes wet, Kaiya could only nod. His words were absolutely true. He would do anything she asked. That included waiting in the background while she decided whether she wanted to continue their relationship. It would be easier to be selfish if he wasn't so understanding. Be that as it may, Kaiya was a student of the wind. She loved Galen, but she wasn't certain it was the same love he felt for her. Would he be content to remain friends for centuries, never expecting more? Or would he eventually decide she wasn't worth his affections and leave her to pursue a new love? Only time would tell, but his loyal nature and cheerful outlook on life would likely stop him from ever turning his back on her.

Gently stroking the side of his face, she sniffled twice before saying, "Your new look is wonderful."

His eyes danced with delight. The two shared a bond that went far beyond the surface. No cosmetic changes could ever change such deep affection.

"This is the kindest thing you could have given me, and I will treasure it." Kaiya couldn't resist an attempt at seeing inside his mind. Not enough to reveal his secrets, but only to glimpse his heart. Though her skill was slight, and his elven mind was well-shielded, she felt a deep sense of love. To her relief, it did not speak of longing or yearning for something more. Galen expected no more from their relationship than what it currently was, and Kaiya found herself at ease.

Disconnecting herself from his mind, she smiled at her friend. Here stood her soul mate, the one who would stand at her side until all things came to an end. The two understood each other in a way that was almost impossible. Whether in this realm or the next, the two would remain together for all time.

A gentle wind made its way through the window and danced upon her skin. Caressing her with its gentle hand, it blessed her with its warmth. Squeezing the stone in her hand, she felt it alive with magical energy—a kiss from the wind to seal the elven magic inside it.

"Were you able to learn any more about the Gawr?" Galen asked.

"Yes," Kaiya said, coming back to reality. "I saw the destruction the Gawr can cause, and I saw the Ancients repairing the damage. Apparently it's a cycle, one that has gone on for millennia."

"Did you find a way control it?" Galen asked.

"I think so," Kaiya replied. "The Ancients visited the Ulihi. I saw it in my vision." To Tashi, she said, "Your people were tasked with keeping the Gawr under control. It was a High Priestess I saw learning from the Ancients."

"This knowledge wasn't passed to me," Tashi said. Searching her mind, she wondered if her mother had been aware of this when she served as High Priestess. If so, she never acted upon it in Tashi's lifetime. "I must make this right."

"You will," Kaiya said. Of that she had no doubt. Reaching for a quill on the table before her, Kaiya drew out the runes she had seen the Ancients scrawl in the dirt. "Do you recognize these?"

Tashi shook her head.

"I do," Galen said. "They translate to silence, stillness, and rest."

"These runes are the key to keeping the Gawr sealed away," Kaiya said. "It must not be allowed to awaken fully. Once it is back asleep, it will stop sending its rock creatures, and the world will be safe."

"Won't it wake again at some point?" Galen asked. "No offense, Tashi, but your people are few, and you said no children have survived infancy. The Ulihi can't be expected to fulfill this obligation for eternity."

"We will survive," Tashi stated firmly. "Neglecting this duty could explain why our gods abandoned us. Once it is complete, our children might survive." For the first time since Annin's death, Tashi felt a glimmer of hope. Maybe this was why the gods ignored her prayers. "Let me come with you," she said to Kaiya. "Whatever you need, I will do it." This could be her chance to atone for her sin. She woke this creature, and now she would send it back to its rest. With luck, it would please the gods and bring the Ulihi back in their favor. Afterward, her people could punish her as they saw fit, likely banning her from the village. As long as her sister's child was safe, then her own fate was irrelevant.

"You may come," Kaiya replied. "I doubt the journey will be easy. We must travel light and leave as soon as possible." Narrowing her eyes at Galen, she asked, "I don't suppose you could save me a trip and carve these runes with enough power to bind the Gawr, could you?"

Galen shook his head. "I wish I could," he said. "Unfortunately, it's far beyond my skill. Even Trin, with his lifetime of experience, doesn't have the power to do something like that." The Ancients had crafted the runes that would subdue the Gawr, and Galen couldn't begin to compare with their power.

"It was worth a try," Kaiya replied with a shrug. She wondered briefly if the elves of the isles, the ones who worked with Dwarf's Heart, might have such skill. Finding out, however, would take far too long, and time was not on her side. The Gawr's power grew daily.

"I'd like to come along as well," the elf announced. Wishing he could justify the desire, he found no good reason for offering his presence.

"You must stay behind," Kaiya insisted. "If we fail, you can reach out to the Westerling Elves. Perhaps they can succeed if we don't."

Despite his desire to protest, Galen knew the journey would be dangerous, and Kaiya would need all her skills focused on completing the task. The last thing she needed was him getting hurt and needing rescue. He had no skills for battle, and his knowledge of the mountains was limited. He would only slow her down. Nodding, he replied, "I will do that. Make sure you come back in one piece."

"That's the plan," Kaiya said, a half-smile appearing on her face. Taking a piece of parchment, she drew a crude map of the areas she had seen in her vision. "Any of these look familiar?" she asked Tashi.

Studying the map a moment, Tashi began to recognize the area. "Yes," she said. "I know of the paths." Handing the map back to Kaiya, she added, "I admit that I've never stood upon those peaks. I can find the path for us, but I can't say what lies at the end of it."

"Luckily I've seen what awaits us," Kaiya said. "Stones containing the runes we require were placed there by the Ancients." The rune stones had to still be there. If they had been destroyed, there was no hope left. She could only trust that the Ulihi had simply forgotten their duty, rather than being forced to abandon it because the runes were no longer available.

"What do we do with the stones?" Tashi asked.

"I will call upon lightning to reignite the runes," the sorceress explained. "Lightning is the world's own energy, and it will rekindle the magic that has faded."

"Then I don't understand how a High Priestess was charged with this task," Tashi replied. "We have no true magic to do as you say."

"I believe you once did," Kaiya replied. "And you will again." The face of Tashi's niece flashed in her mind. "Or at least some of you will."

"Annin's daughter," Tashi whispered. The sorceress's face revealed everything. "She will have the power to do this."

Kaiya gave a single nod as Tashi closed her eyes to process the information. A mixture of pride and sorrow swept over her. Pride in the child who would become what she could not, but sorrow that Annin had not lived to see it. "Magic will return to the Ulihi," she said. "How was it lost? And who was the last to have it?"

"I can't answer that," Kaiya replied. "The wind did not reveal those events to me."

"I don't suppose it matters now," Tashi said. "The future is what matters. We will set this right."

"Be careful, both of you," Galen said. As soon as he spoke the words, he felt foolish, but it was all he could think to say.

"We will," Kaiya promised. "And you be on your guard as well. This camp isn't entirely safe."

Chapter 15

Turning their backs to the mining camp, Kaiya and Tashi began their ascent in search of the first rune stone. A light dusting of snow fell from the sky, soft crystals of ice plinking against the rocky terrain. Kaiya shook her head as she compared her own booted feet to Tashi's bare skin. The two had grown up in the same region under quite different circumstances. It was amazing how the pair could be so different. Even with magic, Kaiya had no desire to walk barefoot through the high elevations. The mere thought sent a shiver through her body.

Seeing her companion's shiver, Tashi tried to reassure her. "The snow will pass soon." Tilting her head skyward, she counted the fast-moving clouds. "No more than fifteen minutes," she said.

Kaiya nodded, content with the estimation, though she wasn't feeling much of the cold. In truth, the only thing she felt was worry that she would not achieve her goal in time. If the Gawr awoke fully, it would take far more power than she possessed to lock him back in his dungeon.

Moving along a high ridge, they reached an iron bridge that would carry them away from the mining camp and into the mountain wilderness. Kaiya hesitated only a moment to glance back toward the city, where life went on as usual. Taking a deep breath, she stepped onto the bridge, a rusty groan releasing itself from the rarely used crossing. A deep chasm lay below them, descending into depths unknown. Paying the drop no heed, the sorceress pressed on, the priestess following close behind.

Safely across the bridge, Kaiya planted her feet firmly in the soft snow. Before she could take another step, the mountain roared to life. A low rumbling, followed by the clanging of boulders echoed across the chasm, the ground quaking in response. Knocked off-balance, Kaiya rolled toward the bridge, slamming her back against the iron rails. Scrambling to her feet, the sound of grinding echoed in her ears. She gritted her teeth against the noise and looked back in time to see the end of the bridge give way.

Tashi grasped at the rails, the bridge teetering precariously. In an instant, it swung free, the continual shaking of the mountain loosening the iron pegs where the bridge was secured. Without thinking, she leapt, hoping desperately to make it to the other side. She failed. Her body hit hard against the edge, her fingers grasping at the edge of the gap.

An unexpected calm settled over the priestess, her fingers freezing in the snow. Looking into the chasm's depths, she felt at peace. Would the fall kill her instantly? Or would she linger, injured, until she finally succumbed? In this moment, the answer mattered not. How easily she could release her grip and make her way back to the arms of her beloved sister. None would mourn her loss. The strength in her hands weakening, and the weight of her body growing heavier, she chose the easiest route—down.

Steadying herself on her knees, Kaiya cursed the incessant shaking. It made concentration extremely difficult. Still, the wind was beside her. The sorceress called it to herself, channeling it through her heart, her eyes flashing silver. The wind obeyed, gusting toward the falling priestess as her hands lost their grip on the ledge. Her focus held firmly upon the spell, Kaiya manipulated the wind, working against the pull of gravity. With a flick of her wrist, she righted the priestess, and guided her upward to solid ground.

Her mind reeling from the fall and sudden rescue, Tashi shook her head to clear it. Kaiya slumped, burying both hands and knees in the snow. Fighting the pull of the world's depths had been no small feat. She would need time to recover, and she welcomed the wind as it comforted her.

Finally, the quaking ceased, the crash of falling rock no longer pounding in their ears. Tashi pulled herself up on her elbows and dared to look down into the gap. *Not yet, Annin,* she thought. Rising to her feet, she moved to the sorceress's side and gently laid a hand on her back. "Are you all right?" she asked.

Kaiya gave a quick nod. "I'll be fine. I just need a few minutes." The wind still swirled around her, quickening her absorption of its power. Its sense of urgency matched her own. "Were you injured?"

"I am fine," Tashi replied, then added, "thanks to you."

Knowing the avalanche would have affected the camp, Tashi climbed higher on the ridge. Squinting her eyes to the distance, she could see the city had been hit hard. Houses had collapsed, and mounds of snow and rock lay piled against what was once a row of shops. Small figures ran in all directions, likely hurrying to aid those who had been injured.

Slowly ascending to Tashi's position, Kaiya also looked upon the destruction. Closing her eyes to the scene, she hung her head in an attempt to hide her tears.

"Should we go back?" Tashi asked. "They might need your help."

Her heart yearned to return. Was Galen injured? And what if the miners were trapped in a cave-in? Magic might be the only way to free them. But the wind whispered a warning, and Kaiya knew the path she must take. "The best help I can give them is to stop the Gawr," she said. "The attacks will only increase if we don't go now." Putting distance between herself and the camp should draw the Gawr's attention away from the innocent. It was her the Gawr wanted, and she would go to it.

"It fears you," Tashi said. "That's why it attacks the city. It hopes to stop you." This was not about her. She woke the Gawr, but Kaiya could force it back to its prison. She was a great threat to the dead god, and Tashi would protect her with her life.

"We have to keep moving," Kaiya replied.

Though concealed beneath layers of avalanche, and the natural decay of time, Tashi easily picked out the pathway once followed by her predecessors. The route was in her blood, a homing instinct to a place she had never visited. How she knew the way, she couldn't explain. Perhaps the spirits of her ancestors revealed the path, guiding her feet along their journey.

"We have to climb here," Tashi said, her eyes scanning the cliffside for a way up.

"There," Kaiya said, using magic to illuminate a worn iron ring, the first of many. The Ulihi had installed a series of thick metal loops to ease their passage to the rune stone. Kaiya couldn't be more grateful. She was no skilled climber, and without the handholds, she would have to resort to magic to make her way upward. The strain on her stores could leave her vulnerable, and there was little chance she wouldn't encounter some resistance. Saving her magic was vital. Though the wind would replenish her, it would take time that she might not have.

Grabbing hold of the loops, Tashi easily pulled herself to the top of the cliff and knelt down to assist Kaiya with her climb. The dwarf made her way up with ease, surprising the priestess. "You're more nimble than you look," she said, smiling. Dwarves were more likely to force change on the mountain than take it as it was. She was pleased that Kaiya had not resorted to magic to make the climb.

As she pulled herself up, Kaiya spotted movement from the corner of her eye. "Look," she whispered, pointing to the right.

Tashi's mouth fell open, her eyes wide with wonder. "A snow cat," she said.

Only steps away from their position, a large white cat with gray and black spots paused to observe the newcomers, its green eyes flashing in the dull light. Staying only a moment, it cared not for the intruders. Powerful muscles rippled as it turned its gaze elsewhere, trotting away to places unknown. Kaiya and

Tashi marveled at its grace as it disappeared among the gray and white backdrop.

"They are extremely rare now," Tashi said, a hint of regret in her voice. Like her own people, these cats had lost much of their territory to dwarven development.

Reaching out, Kaiya attempted to glimpse the cat's mind. There was no malice within it, nor did it feel an urgent need to feed or protect its territory. She let out the breath she'd been holding, content that the snow cat wouldn't be lying in wait for them. To her delight, the cat left tracks, revealing a familiar pathway. This was the area she had seen in her vision. The rune stone had to be nearby.

"It's near," she announced. A slight tingle danced on the end of her nose, alerting her to the presence of magic.

Tashi's eyes drank in the area. Yes, this had to be it. Something told her she was in the right place. But where was the rune stone? Shouldn't it have a place of honor here among the endless sea of stone? Frantically she paced every corner of the small plateau, hoping to find what she sought. Had the ancestors steered her wrong as a punishment? Or was she wrong that they were guiding her? Perhaps that was something she wanted to believe, and they hadn't truly lent their aid. Her hopes sinking, she thought, *I've managed to fool myself, and I've brought Kaiya to the wrong place.*

Carefully choosing her steps, the sorceress followed the magic emanating from the mountain. Stopping before an arched rock formation, she said, "It's buried." Brushing the snow away with her hands, she uncovered a pair of narrow stone doors concealed within the rocks. A thin layer of ice covered the structure, giving it the appearance of a natural formation. This place, however, had been created with care, the work of the Ancients.

Among the ice she found a handle and tugged it. The door protested, but finally opened, revealing a descending stairway. "I have to go down," she said.

Standing at the entrance, Tashi asked, "Can't you cast the lightning from here? You could strike the ground." Wouldn't that be enough power to hit the rune stone beneath them? The forbidding darkness before her sent a chill through her body. Had her ancestors truly visited such a place? The odor of mold and dust found its way into her nostrils, adding to her apprehension.

"It's too deep for the magic to reach," Kaiya replied, a tiny flicker of light dancing on her hand. The staircase turned several times below her, leading deep into the earth. The spell could not be performed from the surface. Sensing Tashi's fear, she said, "You can keep watch over the entrance."

Straightening her back, Tashi replied, "There could be danger down there. I will go below with you." Every fiber of her being implored her to wait at the top, but she could not. If the sorceress was going below, Tashi would follow and protect her from harm at all costs. No other could activate the rune stones should tragedy befall the sorceress.

With her mind fixated on the sky above, Kaiya called forth the lightning. Above her the clouds gathered, darkening to summon their power. A surge of energy unleashed, the heat crackling through the cold mountain air. The sorceress channeled the blast, sparks dancing over her unmoving form. A burst of light erupted in her right hand, spinning and swirling above her palm.

When Kaiya attacked the stone beast in Tashi's village, the priestess had witnessed firsthand the power the sorceress could wield. But seeing the magic fluttering in her hand, Tashi was amazed. Nature itself had come to answer this dwarf's call, obeying her desire to harness its power. This was not the tricks employed by her own profession. This was true magic. Feeling its power so near her, she felt humbled. No need for the gods; elemental magic would save her people. Suppressing a smile, she thought, *The dead god should fear this one.*

An unlit torch awaited the pair as they stepped inside the cavern. Kaiya's captive lightning would provide enough light to see, but once it was spent, the two would be left in darkness. Grabbing the torch, Tashi tipped it toward Kaiya, who allowed a spark to catch the wood. A silver flame burned brightly, its energy vibrating through the handle. Tashi's heart swelled with pride as if she were wielding the magic herself.

Steadying her breathing, Kaiya led the way down the stairs. Maintaining the lightning took an incredible amount of concentration. Should her focus waver, the spell would lose power. There had to be enough left to activate the rune stone, or she'd have to try again. The lack of moving air as she traveled deeper underground unnerved her. With no wind to replenish her magic, she would have to step carefully. There would be no power to spare.

As she descended, dusty webs brushed against Kaiya's face, settling in her hair and wrapping themselves around her arms. Her instinct was to brush them away and look for the creature that had created them, but she could not. All of her focus stayed on the spell in her hand, though the light flickered slightly as she tried to wiggle her nose free of a line of web.

Coming to her aid, Tashi brushed the webs away. "How can spiders stay active in this cold?" she wondered. As the words left her mouth, she wondered if some other creature might live in this place, one that wouldn't be happy to have visitors.

The staircase twisted on, four flights down finally bringing the pair to a lit shrine. Dried reeds thatched together provided a roof, while strips of bark surrounded the rune stone. Granite in color with a painite inlay, the stone had been placed on a pedestal at eye level to an average Ulihi. Nearly square, it measured a foot in both height and width, except for the upper right corner. For some reason it had been chipped away and left uneven.

Holding her torch high, Tashi studied the stone. It was beautiful work, the Dwarf's Heart glistening in the pale light. A shadow moved at the corner of her vision, drawing her attention to the left. Waving the torch, she studied the small, circular chamber. There was no one but her and Kaiya. Listening in the stillness, she heard no living thing, but a slight rotten smell found its way to her nostrils. "I don't like this place," she said. To her, it felt like a place for the dead, where evil spirits might dwell.

"There's nothing here," Kaiya stated, hoping to put her companion's mind at ease. It was a strange sensation. Though she felt the pull of magic from the stone, she sensed nothing else. The Gawr's watchful eyes did not penetrate this place. Was he unaware of it? Or had the Ancients protected it somehow? The answer was unimportant. It was time to activate the stone.

Channeling the power of the lightning, she allowed it to dance upon her fingertips. It had lost some of its charge, but for her first time carrying such power underground, she was impressed at its potency. Thrusting her hand forward, she forced the power into the stone, the painite glistening in response. A charge of magic radiated from the stone, sending a shower of sparks back at her. Standing her ground, she watched as the light grew, the entire cavern illuminated with a deep-red hue. The sight of it nearly took her breath away.

"It's marvelous," Tashi said. Why hadn't she learned of this place before? Why had this work been abandoned, and which of her ancestors was responsible? "My people can't channel lightning," she said. "How will we ever perform this ritual?"

"Once I've reactivated them, keeping them active will be far simpler," Kaiya replied. "But your people once knew this magic, and they will again."

The sorceress had already mentioned that magic would return to the Ulihi, but Tashi still found it hard to believe. "Can you ask the wind why our powers were lost?" she asked. In a flash of understanding, she realized she already knew the answer. "Those who held magic perished, didn't they?" she asked. "They couldn't pass on their gifts." Without them to maintain the rune stones, the Gawr had been left unchecked. That is how Tashi was able to wake it. The realization hit her hard, and she staggered as if struck by a fist.

"I can ask the wind, but it might not know the answer," Kaiya replied. "Your explanation certainly has merit." The dwarves had driven the Ulihi to near extinction, and those with magic were likely the first to go. They would have been targeted by the dwarves, who feared what they did not understand. This was not the time to mention such possibilities to Tashi though. "Come on," she said. "We've got two more of these to find."

At the top of the stairs, Tashi doused the torch in the snow and replaced it on the wall. Future generations might have need of it, at least she hoped they would.

Outside in the moonlight, the snow cat perched itself on a ledge and peered toward the travelers. Its muscles tensed slightly as if it were about to pounce. Instead, it relaxed and stretched itself out on the rocks, the wind tousling its plush fur.

"It knows what we're doing," Kaiya said. "I believe it wishes us safe journeys."

"I think you're right," Tashi replied, fixated on the majestic creature. Its reappearance was a sign of good fortune, a blessing upon their quest.

A rumbling deep within the mountain reminded them both that there was still much work to be done. "The Gawr knows we've reactivated the stone," Kaiya said. If it hadn't been aware of this location before, it certainly was now. The ancient power locked in the stone was no longer hidden. "We must be ever vigilant. Danger could be anywhere."

Chapter 16

Under the shimmering light of the moon, Kaiya turned her gaze back toward the encampment. Fear shivered through her body as she looked upon the mountains silhouetted against the stars. It was time to ask the question she had been too afraid to ask. Projecting her mind to the wind, she asked, *Does Galen live?*

A gentle breeze touched her cheek but gave no answer. Shivering against the cold, she waited. Was the answer too terrible for the wind to pronounce? *I must know,* she said, pleading.

Stillness replied. Could she continue if he was gone? Would the world still be worth saving? A frigid tear rolled down her cheek, soon dried by the wind's gentle kiss.

He lives, the wind replied.

A mixture of relief and elation ran through her mind, her face turned upward to the stars. Galen had indeed survived the avalanche. The Gawr had not taken its anger at her out on him. For fear of the answers, she asked no more questions. It was time to press on and complete her mission.

Pointing to the westward sky, Tashi said, "There's a storm coming." The stars hid themselves behind a dense layer of cloud. A heavy snowfall was imminent. "Can you stop it?" she asked.

"No," Kaiya replied. "I can't."

Tashi stared at her in disbelief. "Surely the power is within you."

"It's one thing to manipulate the wind," she explained. "It's quite another to stop it entirely."

"So you can't do it?" Tashi asked. "I saw you call lightning from the clouds."

"That energy was already there," the dwarf explained. "I only channeled it. I could probably deflect the storm from my body, but I couldn't stop it from its purpose."

After a moment of thought, Tashi said, "I like that."

"You like that?" Kaiya didn't understand.

"That you have limits," the priestess went on.

Shrugging, Kaiya said, "I imagine limitless power would have its benefits."

"Those without limits manipulate all around them, like the gods," Tashi replied. "They do what is best for them, not the people they are supposed to protect. That does not describe you." In her eyes, Kaiya was far better than the gods. The dwarf woman would risk her own life to save others, though the danger had yet to reach her own home. She had traveled toward the danger to protect the miners and also Tashi's people, once she knew of their existence. The gods were never so selfless.

"You might be right about the gods," Kaiya said. "I don't know much about them. My people don't typically give much thought to religion. It is said the dwarves created themselves, carving our own bodies out of the mountain."

Laughing, Tashi said, "Maybe they did." Her mood lighter, she tried not to think of the harm the dwarves had caused her people. Kaiya was not of the same mind as those who had wronged the Ulihi. Perhaps not all dwarves were alike. Many among them might share Kaiya's opinion. "Will you go to visit your king after this is finished?" she asked.

"If I survive, that is the first place I'll go," Kaiya replied. "Well, after I visit my parents, of course. They still worry about me." She dared not ask the wind whether her parents were safe. A negative answer might prove too painful to bear, and it would hinder her ability to focus on her magic. With luck, the Gawr would never achieve the power to fully attack her home village.

Tilting her head, Tashi directed Kaiya to a ledge. "We need to drop down here," she said, sitting and sliding herself over the edge.

The sorceress followed suit. "The next rune stone is the farthest from the mines," she said.

Snow began to fall, light at first but becoming heavier as they moved. The wind increased, chilling the travelers, even the priestess whose people were acclimated to such conditions. The long walk and urgency with which they moved had stolen some of Tashi's strength, leaving her more vulnerable to the weather. Her spirit undaunted, she led on, seeking out the path of her ancestors.

When the moon disappeared behind the clouds, Kaiya summoned a small sphere of light in her hand. Offering it to Tashi, she said, "You're the leader. You should carry the light."

Holding out her hand, Tashi allowed the sorceress to place the magic in her palm. Lines of white and silver swirled before her eyes, nearly hypnotizing her with their beauty. The spell emitted little heat—enough to warm but not burn. Kaiya summoned a second sphere and held onto it, both spells sustaining themselves by the energy of the gusting wind.

"Promise me you will teach my niece to do this," Tashi said.

"To create light?" Kaiya asked.

"Yes, and also to perform this ritual with the rune stones," the priestess replied. "She must learn to keep our people safe throughout her lifetime. Someday she will serve as High Priestess, and I would have her learn this task directly from you." She swallowed hard. The request depended on whether they succeeded in their endeavor. If the world came to an end at the hands of the Gawr, there would be no Ulihi to protect.

"I'd be honored," Kaiya replied.

"I cannot thank you enough for what you are doing," Tashi said. "I caused this, and you are making it right."

Pausing, Kaiya reached out to her companion. "You didn't cause this," she said. "There is no ritual that wakes the Gawr. With no one maintaining the rune stones that bind it to its sleep, it simply wakes during certain cycles."

Her brow wrinkling as if in pain, Tashi nodded. Above all, she wanted to believe Kaiya's words, but she could not. She knew the ritual to summon the dead god was banned for a reason—she had learned that lesson all too well. If it helped Kaiya to think better of her, she would not try to convince her otherwise. Her guilt was her own to carry.

Darkness enveloped the mountains, save for the illumination of Kaiya's magic as it glinted off the rapidly falling snowflakes. A crunchy layer of icy snow accumulated at their feet, soon making its way to their ankles. If only she could stop the storm, Kaiya's feet would be warm. She hoped Tashi wasn't suffering too much, but the Ulihi woman showed no sign of discomfort. Despite her lack of shoes, her thick feet provided her with ample protection. Kaiya envied her companion as she wiggled her own toes to keep the blood circulating. Magic would warm them, but she feared overdrawing her reserves.

In the same instant, both women spotted a firelight glowing in the distance. "Who would make camp this high in the mountains?" Tashi wondered. None but the Ulihi used these paths, and they showed no signs of anyone traversing them recently.

"Looks like we're about to find out," Kaiya replied. Holding her light forward, she could see the path ahead, and it ran directly toward the fire.

Proceeding with caution, the pair approached the campsite before them. Seven humanoid shapes sat upon rocks circled around the fire. Two held sticks in their hands, extending them over the flames. A faint scent of cooked meat wafted toward the travelers.

"Could they be dwarves?" Tashi asked.

Kaiya shook her head. "Too skinny," she replied. Never in her life had she seen a dwarf who wasn't stocky. These figures had long arms, proportionally long for their height, though they stood no taller than her. Reaching into her magical stores, she attempted to touch the mind of the nearest one. Pulling back quickly, she said, "Goblins."

"They live here?" Tashi asked. She had heard of them in tales, but they always lived in caves or dark corners of the forest.

"I'm guessing they've found some type of shelter up here," Kaiya said. She had not expected to see goblins at this elevation either. They normally preferred warmer climates, but here they were. The real question was, were they going to cause a problem?

"Maybe we should go around them," Tashi suggested. Goblins were not know to be friendly, and the pair were in a hurry.

"No," Kaiya replied. "We're going through them." Going around would take too long. Any obstacle in her way would have to be surmounted. The goblins would allow her passage, or she would make them regret it.

Their yellow eyes gleaming in the firelight, the goblins took notice of the women as they drew nearer. They rose to their feet, maintaining a slightly hunched posture.

"We don't want any trouble," Kaiya announced. "We only wish to pass through, and you can go right back to your meal."

"Pretty lady," one goblin said as he moved near Tashi.

The priestess recoiled as the green-gray skinned creature came near, the scent of musk and rotting leaves assaulting her nose.

Leaning in toward her, the goblin reached its fingers for her beaded necklace. "Shiny," it said as it tugged on the beads.

Raising her staff, Tashi whacked the goblin on its arm. Grabbing its bruised skin, it stepped backward and stared at the woman.

"Witch," it said, a gnarled finger pointing at Tashi.

"No," Kaiya said. "I'm the witch." With a snap of her fingers, sparks danced upon the palm of her hand. "Now leave us in peace."

The goblins scattered, their feet skittering like roaches in the snow. Squealing and squawking, they circled around the travelers, muttering words of nonsense that might have been their native tongue.

Slinking toward the women, the goblins attempted to close the circle, their yellow eyes menacing. Five creatures took on an attack posture, the other two hanging back with looks of uncertainty.

Sighing, Kaiya prepared herself for an attack. "There's a greater danger in these mountains than us," she said, attempting to reason with them. "My mission is to protect you as well as everyone else. Don't be stupid. Just let us pass."

Continuing to whoop and squawk, the goblins closed in. Tashi prepared her blowgun, striking before the goblins were too close. She hit one in its eye, forcing it to cry out in pain, cradling its face in its hands.

While the others looked on in shock at their injured friend, Kaiya took advantage. Manipulating the swirling snow, she fashioned a whip with several long lashes of ice. Striking the goblins, they shrieked with pain. They scattered, fleeing in all directions, pursued by the lashes. Kaiya struck blow after blow, her eyes flashing silver with each strike.

Shrieking into the darkness, the goblins disappeared down the mountainside. It was almost comical, and Kaiya would have laughed if she had the time. Right now she had no patience for goblin stupidity. "Let's go before they come back," she said.

Goblins were notorious for not knowing when they were beaten.

"Why didn't you kill them?" Tashi wondered. She felt no mercy for the menacing creatures, but she doubted the one she had darted would die from its injuries. Still, it was unlikely the goblin would ever forget what had happened—its eye would have to be removed.

"They're ignorant little thieves, but I don't wish death upon them." Kaiya replied. "And I doubt they planned to kill us." Tashi's attack had angered them, and they might have wanted to harm the women, but Kaiya knew they were no match for her.

The storm broke after midnight, but the damage had already been done. Over a foot of snow slowed travel for the diminutive pair, who both stood less than four feet in height. Tashi moved as if she felt no cold, but Kaiya was quickly becoming fed up. Her woolen cloak remained dry, warming her top half, but her legs in their leather wrappings were wet and cold. With no other choice, she used her magic, drawing the water away from her body and releasing it into the air. The spell would have to be repeated as she walked, but it was worth the toll on her magical stores. The boost to her morale was immeasurable.

It was a full day's march before Kaiya felt the familiar twinge of magic running through her veins. "The rune stone is near," she announced.

"There," Tashi said, pointing straight ahead. A small shrine of piled smooth stones sheltered the ancient artifact from the elements. Near its base, she spotted a pile of bones. Kneeling next to them, she said, "These are Ulihi." She lifted a delicate strand of beads for the sorceress to observe.

"Is this how your people bury the dead?" she asked.

Shaking her head, Tashi said, "We burn our dead and collect the bones for burial. This person must have died here."

"Then who arranged the bones?" Kaiya asked. The body was arranged in a seated position, the skeleton reclining slightly against the rocks, its leg bones crossed, its hands neatly tucked within its ribcage. It was unlikely someone had died in that position.

"I don't know," Tashi replied. "Maybe two people came here, and only one was able to return."

"Perhaps it was a High Priestess, and she wished to be placed here," Kaiya suggested. Whoever this person was, he or she was far beyond help. Drawing energy through her body, Kaiya focused her mind to the clouds above. They came together on a heavy wind, charging their power and flashing with a silver light. Directing the energy toward the stone, sparks flew from her fingertips. In a flash of white fire, the lightning slammed into the stone. The Dwarf's Heart rune illuminated in response.

The mountain beneath them roared in anger, the creature trapped within enraged at their actions. A deep groan reverberated among the stones, the Gawr's malice unleashed upon the world. Chunks of ice and snow, some of them large enough to flatten a village, broke free of the mountainside and plummeted downward.

A shiver of fear ran through the sorceress. Had the Gawr come to full power? A kiss from the wind reassured her it had not. If the Gawr had regained all its strength, it could collapse the mountain upon her. No, she still had time.

Seeing the danger above them, Tashi grabbed Kaiya's arm and pulled her back toward the path. "Run!" she shouted.

Sliding from the summit, an avalanche of white aimed itself at the travelers, its intent clear. A mind of hatred spurred it onward, targeting the sorceress who would see its master undone. Gaining speed as it fell, hundreds of pounds of ice and snow rushed toward the women. Death and destruction rained upon them, pushed by the hand of evil.

Racing at top speed, the pair desperately tried to outrun their pursuer. Kaiya ran more slowly than Tashi, but the priestess had not let go of her arm, dragging the sorceress forward with all her might. A constant rumbling accompanied their footsteps, loosening the rock beneath them. Kaiya slipped on the rubble, sending her sliding past Tashi. To her amazement, she came to a stop at a plateau, right before the edge of a cliff.

"It's sheltered!" she called out. "We can drop down here!"

When she looked back at Tashi, the priestess had disappeared, buried beneath a blanket of white. The raging snow continued on its path, sweeping Kaiya over the edge. Digging into her magical stores, she called out to the wind, riding its soft embrace over the cliff. Flattening herself against the edge of the cliff, she looked up at the rocky overhang above her. The pair could have made it to safety within seconds but had failed. Now Tashi lay buried beneath the snow.

Chapter 17

Digging with bare hands, Galen frantically clawed through the rubble. His heart sank as he reached the girl he sought. Her yellow hair was caked with crimson blood, her face cold to the touch. Gently pressing his fingers to her neck, he found no pulse. No more than fourteen years of age, this sweet life had been cut short by the Gawr's wrath.

Sitting back on his heels, the elf hung his head. This was the second avalanche to strike since Kaiya departed days ago. The first had caused serious injuries but no deaths. This one had killed dozens of citizens and destroyed several homes. The schoolhouse was demolished, but thankfully the children had not been inside. Their teacher took them underground at the first hint of rumbling. The poor child lying before Galen had been a worker. Had she still been in school, she would have been safe.

Pulling her free of the rubble, he placed her on top of the rocks and folded her hands across her abdomen. Here she would wait for the wagons that collected the dead.

Such senseless waste of life weighed heavily on the elf, and he did not bother to hide his tears. Reinforced with steel, the Dwarf's Heart workshop was the safest place in the encampment. That is where Galen had been when the chaos began. His only injury was a minor scrape on his forehead. Along with the others, he ran outside as soon as the shaking subsided. An eerie silence greeted him—no wails of despair nor grief. Instead of mourning, the dwarves had gone to work, digging at the earth to free their trapped loved ones.

The mines had been evacuated days earlier, shortly after Kaiya took her leave. She had gone to challenge the Gawr, and in his wisdom, Foreman Daro had insisted the workers stay away. There was more than enough work for them to do in the city, where they used their skills to unearth fallen dwarves and construct temporary shelters for the newly homeless.

What these people needed most were healers. Galen had no such skills, but other elves did. Unfortunately, he had no way to summon them, and he could not leave now. The dwarves needed every pair of hands they could get. He had never learned healing runes, but they had to exist. Many dwarves lay comatose with head injuries, using the strength of their own bodies to heal themselves. They might benefit from a rune carver's help. The girl before him was beyond such things.

His head low, he stumbled back to the workshop, the coppery smell of blood unsettling his stomach. Resisting the urge to wretch, he stepped inside the shop and found himself alone. Grabbing a set of tools, he poured himself into his work. Runic symbols flashed in his mind, none of them adequate for healing. Frustrated, he chipped at the stones, reviewing his early lessons by starting at the top of the list. Running through the alphabet, he recalled every ancient rune he knew. Still he came up empty.

Before he realized what he had done, seven small stones lay on the table before him. Smoothed and ready for their enchantments, he stared at them as if they would offer the answer. Slamming a fist against the table, he cursed the city. There were no archives nor library, things essential for his work. How could he learn which runes to etch if he had no guide? Knowledge was worth more than painite. Didn't the dwarves realize this?

Sighing, Galen buried his head in his hands. Dirt from the stones transferred to his face, adding to his already disheveled look. *Healing stones,* he repeated to himself. Another sigh, this one cursing his own failure rather than the dwarves' lack of interest in libraries. Placing his forehead against the table, he closed his eyes.

In a flash of remembrance, the runic symbol for repair came into his mind. Normally, it was etched into weapons, protecting them from a certain amount of damage. But it was usually inlaid with diamond or ruby, and he had none available. Could such an enchantment work for people? He had no idea, but it might be worth a try.

The rune for rejuvenation was commonly placed on jewelry to aid weary soldiers on long marches or in combat. Galen had never heard of it for actual healing, but wouldn't that also help? He wanted to slap himself for forgetting. These runes had potential, all he lacked were diamonds. The ladies of the town might give up their jewels, but they would take time to collect. He'd have to go around, asking grieving widows and mothers to give up their possessions, while all he had was an idea in return. It might not work at all.

Glancing around the room, he saw glimmers of painite on every desk. The dwarves had left in the middle of their work, the precious gemstones cast aside in the wake of such devastation. They knew what was more important, and so did the elf. Racing around the room, he gathered as many pieces as he could. Some were incredibly small, but all had purpose. Never before had he studied the magical properties of Dwarf's Heart, but if it held any at all, he would find out.

Without thought for the great amount of wealth to be had from these gems, he cut them and shaped them, placing each meticulously inside the stones. When he ran out of stones, he turned to chunks of iron and pieces of wood, anything that was close at hand. As he worked nonstop, he thought of other enchantments that might help as well: strength, rest, purify, sharpen. Something had to have medicinal value. It was all the elf had to offer.

It was hours before he declared himself finished, at least for the moment. He had plenty to distribute, and it was time to find out if his creations would work. Bundling the runed items in a canvas sack, he ran out of the workshop and sprinted through the city. Several buildings were now serving as hospitals, and he stepped inside the nearest one.

Foreman Daro stood inside. He turned and gave the elf a half-smile, all he could muster. "Good to see you safe," he said.

"Here," Galen said, handing Daro one of the stones. "I've crafted these with elven magic, and I think they might help the wounded."

Daro had long believed in the power of elves, and his eyes lit up at the prospect. "What do we do with them?"

"Distribute them to those in need," Galen replied. "I'm not sure which will work best, or what conditions will benefit most, so hand them out at random. If they work, we'll know soon."

"Is this Dwarf's Heart?" Daro asked, squinting at the stone.

"It is," Galen replied. He hoped the foreman would not be angered or accuse him of theft.

"They'll be worth a fortune if they work," the dwarf commented. "They're already worth a fortune, but no telling how much those island elves will pay for healing stones of Dwarf's Heart."

"I don't know what properties the painite has," Galen admitted. "But we still have to try. We should place them beneath the pillows of the injured."

He passed a fair amount of the runes to Daro, who obeyed eagerly. When they had placed an enchantment under each pillow, they walked together to the next hospital. No dwarves questioned the pair, instead they barely took notice. The two were uninjured, and there were plenty of ailing dwarves to care for. Two healthy individuals visiting the patients were the least of their concerns.

As they exited a third hospital, Daro said, "I sure hope those work. We could use a miracle about now."

"We should send word to the Vale," Galen replied. "It will be days before they arrive, but there are skilled healers among my people. I know they'd be willing to help."

"I'll do that," Daro said. As soon as he could locate a runner who hadn't been hurt, he would set him to the task.

"Master Elf!" a voice cried. A young boy ran toward them. When he reached the pair, he leaned heavily against his thighs, panting. "Come and see," he managed to say.

"See what?" Galen asked.

"The runes, sir," the boy replied. "My papa is awake!" A broad smile spread across the boy's face. Taking the elf's hand, he pulled him back toward the hospital.

Sitting up in bed was the injured father, a bloodstained bandage wrapped around his head. He nodded at the approach of his young son.

"It was your gift," the boy said. "Papa's all better." The boy grabbed onto Galen's legs and hugged him.

"Not completely better," the injured dwarf said. "But better than I was. Thank you, Master Elf." He inclined his head slightly in appreciation.

"My pleasure," Galen said. "What was your injury? How do you feel?"

"I was hauling a cart up near the mines," the dwarf replied. "I heard the thunder and decided to make a run for it. The cart was struck, and boards came flying. I guess one got me."

"He was out cold," the boy continued. "The doc told me not to expect him to wake. Said his brain was swelling and he'd likely die." He looked up at the elf. "But then you came with your magic trinkets, and now look at him!" The child beamed ear to ear.

Galen wasn't sure if it was the runes that had helped the man, but he was glad to see even one patient recover. Too many had not.

"Look!" Daro said, pointing to another patient.

The man stirred in his bed, groggy, but alive. He was bandaged across his head as well as his arms and one leg.

"That's Arly," Daro said, moving toward the man. "He was crushed. No hope at all, the doc said." He waved to catch the doctor's attention. "He's waking."

The doctor examined his patient, and said, "He has internal injuries. He shouldn't still be breathing." Dwarf doctors were not known for having a gentle nature. They did not sugarcoat a diagnosis.

His eyes opening, the man struggled to sit up. Aided by Daro, Arly looked around the room. "What happened?" he asked.

"Rockslide," Daro said. "You were hurt."

"I saw it coming," Arly said. "Figured I was a goner. My head is ringing, but I think I might live after all."

Galen reached under the dwarf's pillow and pulled out the enchanted item. It was a small piece of iron, engraved with a painite rune. "Balance," he said, reading the rune. Could this have saved Arly's life?

"I don't believe it," the doctor said, his voice barely more than a whisper. As he looked around the room, dozens of patients were sitting upright.

"You've done it!" Daro shouted, clapping the elf on the back.

"We'll have to inspect the runes and see which ones are working," Galen said. Then he could re-create the enchantments that worked best for healing.

One dwarf sputtered and coughed, the doctor rushing to his aid. He tended the man only briefly before covering his face with a sheet. He pulled the rune from under the pillow and handed it to the elf.

"Balance," Galen read, furrowing his brow. Why did it work for one and not the other? The dwarf in the next bed sat up, still in pain but alive. Galen reached under the pillow and drew out the runed item. "Strength," he said. He did not understand.

"Is that what brought me back?" the dwarf asked.

"I'm not sure," Galen answered.

"Well, I do feel strong," the man said, looking the elf in the eye.

Galen replaced the rune under the man's pillow and began checking the others. A variety of runes had produced an effect, though none completely healed any patient. A few more patients breathed their last, their runes being a random assortment as well. Perhaps they were too far gone for his own weak magic to help. It was also possible that his runes had done nothing, and the patients had simply healed on their own. He could not know without further study.

"For what it's worth," Daro said, "I think you did a fine job. Your work here has saved many lives."

Galen remained unconvinced. "Maybe," he said.

The doctor approached in silence and handed Galen another runed trinket, taken from the bed of a dead woman.

Galen's heart sank as he read the enchantment. "Strength." He was no closer to finding a solution. If he didn't know which runes worked, he couldn't use the same for everyone.

"She was nearly gone when they brought her in," the doctor said. "Most of the patients who are now wide awake shouldn't have lived. Don't beat yourself up, Master Elf. You can't save them all."

"That won't stop me from trying," Galen said. As he stared at the rune, he noticed imperfections in the painite that he hadn't seen before. In his rush to craft the enchantments, he hadn't bothered to check the quality of the gems. "The gemstones are flawed," he said.

Daro took the stone and examined it closely. "Those must have been castoffs," he said. "Where did you get the gems?"

"I picked up everything that was lying around the workshop," the elf replied.

"Even the ones in the wire baskets?" Daro asked.

Galen nodded.

"Those are the castoffs," Daro explained. "The elves won't buy them because they have too many flaws."

"Because they won't hold an enchantment," Galen said, realizing his mistake. The Enlightened Elves prided themselves on their ability to enchant any item, no matter how mundane. It was the purity of the gemstones that held the spell, and they were masters of their craft. Now Galen felt lower than an apprentice. "I failed them," he said. The lives lost were his fault.

"No," Daro replied. "You did what you could. There weren't enough perfect gems there to work with. It was better to try the flawed ones than nothing at all."

Nodding slowly, Galen said, "I suppose you're right." He had used every speck of painite in the workshop, no matter how small. Those who received the flawless gems would recover. The others might not be so lucky. His mind turned to Kaiya and the rune stone he'd given her. "The gems I bought for Kaiya, were they flawless?"

"Of course," Daro replied. "That was a good trade. You won't get any tricks out of me. Elf hair of that quality was worth the finest painite I could find."

Galen took solace in those words. At the very least, Kaiya's rune stone should function properly. That was assuming he had crafted it correctly. The painite was difficult to work with, and that had been his first attempt.

"What happens if we take the working trinkets from the dwarves who are starting to recover?" Daro asked. "We could use them for the ones who haven't woke yet."

"That's a brilliant idea," Galen said, wondering why he hadn't thought of it. Even if the patients weren't fully recovered, they were better off than many others who were still lying unconscious. Maybe the runes could not heal them, but it could help them on their way.

The two busied themselves swapping out enchanted items and inspecting them for their quality. By the time they had revisited all three hospitals, most of the patients were beginning to recover. All still had a long road ahead of them, but the Dwarf's Heart had worked its magic. No more lives would be lost.

"Now, can you carve us something that will prevent more rockslides?" Daro asked.

"I wish I could," Galen replied.

"Then maybe you can make us men strong enough to hold back the mountain when it starts crashing down again." Daro knew the comment was silly. If the elf had that kind of power, they wouldn't be in this mess in the first place.

Galen's only response was to look at the dwarf and sigh. "I have a lot more studying to do," he said. "I wish there were books here, old ones."

"You'll have to travel to the king's library," Daro said. "The Royal University is the only place in all the mountains where you can study any subject besides metallurgy. We don't have many scholars around here, in case you couldn't tell." He smiled at the elf, hoping to ease his burden. "You've already done a lot for us, and your friend is out there trying to fix the rest."

"I'd like to see that library," Galen said. If Kaiya was successful, he just might get the chance. Dwarf's Heart had magical properties, and it was likely the Enlightened Elves knew what they were. He would need to travel to their islands as well, once his studies among the dwarves were finished. Bringing this knowledge to the world would be his life's work.

Runes held more power than anyone had imagined. More than enchantments for weapons and tools, they had the potential to make the world whole again. It was a lesson the Ancients had tried to teach their descendants when they used runes to subdue the Gawr. Too many centuries had passed, and too much had been forgotten, but the mountain itself remembered.

Chapter 18

Kaiya remained still, holding her body as close to the cliff as she could. For what seemed an eternity, massive quantities of snow and ice continued to rain down. She hoped the overhang was strong enough to withstand the barrage. Otherwise, she too might find herself buried alive.

Finally the rumbling stopped, as did the sliding snow. Scrambling back up the cliff, Kaiya found herself knee-deep in white, surprisingly less than she had expected. The momentum of the avalanche had forced most of the bulk over the edge, leaving the area traversable.

Somewhere beneath the ice lay Tashi, and Kaiya would not leave her behind. A flash of silver swirled in her eyes, sparks appearing in her upturned palms. Reaching out for the priestess's mind, she located her missing companion. Targeting the snow that concealed her, she unleashed the heat in her hands. Layer by layer the snow melted away, revealing a beaded headdress.

Ceasing her spell, Kaiya dropped to her knees and brushed the snow away. It was Tashi, and she was in one piece. Placing her head to her chest, she heard the sound of a beating heart. Cradling her companion in her arms, she forced the heat from the air and channeled it through Tashi's body.

A surge of warmth came over the priestess, her muscles aching as they thawed. Her eyes opened to see a mass of purple hair swirling on the wind. She pulled herself away from the sorceress. "I am alive," she said, stunned.

"Yes, you are," Kaiya replied.

"You came back for me," the priestess said. She was insignificant. Only Kaiya's journey mattered. "Why did you not go on?"

"Because I had to find you," Kaiya answered, confused. Why shouldn't she return for her companion and guide? The two had developed a friendship, at least she felt they had. "I couldn't live with myself if I left a friend behind."

"What if I had been dead?" Tashi wondered.

"You weren't," Kaiya replied. "Can you walk?"

Tashi nodded. Taking in her surroundings, she said, "We've lost the path." All around her was buried in a fresh layer of snow. One area looked identical to the next.

"We need to descend a bit," Kaiya said. "After that, I'll have to rely on the wind to point us in the right direction." The wind had given her the vision of the locations she was to visit, so it had to know the quickest way to get there. "Hold onto my arm," she said.

Silver magic engulfed the women as they stood side by side. "We have to step over the edge," Kaiya said. "Hang onto me, and don't be frightened."

To her surprise, Tashi felt no fear. Together the pair stepped off the cliff's edge, and should have plummeted to their demise. But an invisible force guided their descent, cradling them as they flew. *This must be what it feels like to ride upon the clouds,* Tashi thought.

Twenty or thirty minutes passed, Tashi could not be sure. Still they floated along, drifting eastward. The landscape before her became familiar, and she knew the rune stone drew near. Finally, the wind placed the women gently on the ground, both needing a moment to regain their balance.

"Could you have used this magic to take us to the summit?" Tashi wondered. It had taken some time to travel on foot, time that could have been saved had they used the wind for travel.

"Working against gravity takes a lot more power than working with it," Kaiya replied. "So the short answer is no." Even a mistress of air had her limits.

"I see the path," Tashi said, inclining her head. "It might take two days, maybe more, to reach the rune stone."

"That will give me time to recover," Kaiya said. The Gawr was angry, and it wasn't going down without a fight. If her stores were replenished by then, she might stand a chance against her foe.

A slow march lay ahead of them, with piles of debris—both small and large—hindering their progress. Neither complained, but both longed to find the third rune stone and complete their mission. Every obstacle felt like a nail through Kaiya's body, but she gritted her teeth and pressed on. The journey would not break her.

With the wind at their backs, they followed the path, straying at times to avoid debris. Tashi mourned the loss of a copse of evergreens, hundred-year-old trees flattened by the Gawr's wrath. These trees provided homes for birds and furred creatures, and had earned the respect of her people. The Gawr had no right to harm them.

Nearly three days passed before the travelers came within sight of their destination. Neither had slept more than an hour at a time, instead choosing to use small bursts of magic to revitalize them. It was a small price to pay, and the wind graciously stayed by Kaiya's side, feeding her the power she needed to continue.

Cautiously following the path to the rune stone, the priestess could smell danger. "It's guarded," she said, barring Kaiya's path.

Kaiya already knew. She sensed the magic of the stone, as well as the presence of creatures conjured by dark magic. A tingle ran through her body, and she shuddered, knowing a fight lay ahead. "How many do you see?" she asked.

"Many," Tashi replied. "They have the shrine surrounded. At least five of them, creatures of stone." Barely able to believe her eyes, she looked upon the beasts. Two stood on four legs, one on three, and a biped stood guard at the end of the path. Another sat low to the ground, with what appeared to be several appendages along each side of its elongated torso. "I will distract them," she offered. "When they come for me, you can call down the lightning."

Kaiya admired her friend's bravery. "It's far too dangerous," she said. Besides, the beasts were looking for a sorceress. Tashi wouldn't fool them for long. The Gawr would know who the real threat was, and it would direct its minions to Kaiya. "Try to stay behind me, and watch out for any flying debris," she warned.

Turning her palms upward, she reached into the power of the wind. Sparks flew from her fingertips as she loosed a blast of energy toward the rock beasts. The counterforce of the blast unsteadied her, but she fought it, remaining on her feet. A flash of silver in her eyes, she watched as the spell flew forward.

No effect.

The wave passed over the creatures with a blurring of the light, but it did not faze them. Still as statues, they remained unharmed. Kaiya looked at her hands, wondering if she'd made a mistake. Shaking the thought away, she tried again, this time calling to the skies. The clouds rushed together, darkening and flashing with power. Two bolts of lightning, one immediately following the other, landed in the midst of the stone beasts. Snow and rubble freed by the blast pelted the beasts, but still they remained unmoving, their cold demeanor unshaken.

"They've grown stronger," Tashi whispered. "You have to get near the rune stone. Let me help you."

Taking in a deep breath, Kaiya reluctantly agreed. If the rune were activated, the Gawr might begin to weaken, as would his creations. "This will protect you," she said. Summoning her power, she cast a shield of silver to protect her friend from harm. It was only a temporary measure, and it could be broken, but it was the best protection she could offer.

"I'll get their attention while you make it to the rune stone," Tashi said. Looking toward her enemy, she saw her own fear. A shudder raced through her body, but she forced it away. *I must do this,* she told herself, the face of Annin's child coming to the front of her mind. The child's future was at stake.

265

Moving in a wide arc, Tashi ran toward the beasts, nearing each one before pulling away. The magic of her shield caught their attention, drawing them away from their fixed positions. Their movements clumsy, Tashi felt a surge of confidence. She was nimble and quick. These lumbering hulks could not catch her.

Weaving between the legs of the tall biped, she darted off to the left. Its arm came down far too late— she had already made it to safety. Somersaulting beneath a quadruped, she drew it away from the rune stone. With an exhilarated leap, she landed on the back of the centipede creature, its torso twisting violently in an attempt to shake her off. The quadruped in pursuit tripped on one of the centipede's legs, but Tashi hurried on, sprinting to a safe distance. Behind her she heard a crash as the beasts fell, entangled.

Tashi continued her flight, a proud smile on her face. All of the beasts were in pursuit, save the two who still struggled to right themselves. From the corner of her eye, she glimpsed her companion dashing toward the rune stone, sparks flying from her fingertips.

The presence of strong magic forced the rock beasts away from their prey, their new target identified. Tashi shouted and threw herself among them, hoping to draw their attention, but to no avail. Bound for the sorceress, the creatures had no further interest in Tashi.

Ignoring everything but the rune stone, Kaiya approached the pillar. A single chipped stone stood perched at the top of an obelisk. Its position was impossible, held in place by an unseen force. There was no time to investigate. Unleashing the magic in her hands, Kaiya slammed the rune with a blast of lightning, its deep-red center erupting in a firestorm. A flame of red light burst from the stone, two lines forming in the direction of the other runes. For miles it stretched, connecting the three points of power. Red fire pulsated along each beam of light, the sorceress's bones rattling in response. Ancient magic had been unleashed, and it buried itself inside her soul.

Sprinting toward her was Tashi, her shield entirely depleted. She quickly caught her breath and shouted, "We're trapped!" The beasts had them surrounded.

"No," Kaiya replied, anger flashing in her eyes. Planting her feet firmly in the snow, she focused her mind to the red lights extending from the rune. Summoning her magic, her eyes flashed red.

The stone beasts, oblivious to the danger, continued their approach. As they closed in, Kaiya unleashed her fury. Blasting energy into the lights, she tapped into the magic of the Ancients. A massive explosion threw her backward.

In a flash of red, the rock beasts were struck. Bursting on impact, their forms shattered sending fragments of stone raining down on the sorceress. Her skin stung from repeated impacts as the rubble continued to rain. Shielding her eyes, she scanned the area for Tashi, who had been tossed in the opposite direction.

Kaiya scrambled toward the rune to find Tashi already back on her feet. A deep groaning sound echoed in their ears, the two women clutching each other as they stared straight ahead. The wind swirled before them, gaining speed and lifting the shattered pieces of the stone beasts into the air. Kaiya did not understand. How could the Gawr manipulate the wind? Why would it obey? The answers would have to wait.

Faster and faster the cyclone swirled, smashing stones against the mountainside and reducing them to dust. The pair dropped to their knees to avoid being crushed.

"Can you stop it?" Tashi shouted.

In her mind Kaya pleaded with the wind. Holding her palms outward, she demanded the cyclone stop. It did not. A flash of silver projected from her eyes, the veins in her head throbbing. Pulling deep into her magical stores, she forced the wind to obey. The cyclone continued to whirl, but it held its distance, moving away from the crouched pair.

A warm trickle of blood slid from Kaiya's nose, making its way to her lips. Pain reverberated through her body, her heart pounding in her chest. Feeling as if her lungs would burst, the sorceress began to cough. "I can't hold it," she choked out.

Seeing her friend's distress, Tashi yanked the sorceress to safety behind the pillar where the rune stone still burned brightly. Unhindered, the cyclone renewed its fury, striking the pillar and pounding it with stones.

"What if the pillar is destroyed?" Tashi shouted over the roar of the wind.

Leaning on one elbow, Kaiya lifted her hand. This had to end, one way or another. She did not know if the pillar could survive the barrage; it was up to her to protect it. With her remaining magic, she forced the air around her into an oval-shaped shield. It glowed with a dim silver light, her stores draining fast. With barely enough strength left to stand, she allowed her companion to pull her to her feet.

Tashi's dark eyes looked into Kaiya's, both knowing what they had to do. With a single nod, the priestess stepped within the shield and pulled her companion close. In a quick motion, she forced them both into the path of the Ancient magic.

Red and silver sparks exploded in all directions, the two women flying over the edge of the plateau and tumbling down the mountainside. The cyclone was hit in a massive explosion, sending out a shower of blood-red dust that stained the snow for a mile in all directions. The rune stone remained unharmed.

Groaning in pain, Kaiya could barely move. Every muscle and bone ached, the absolute exhaustion of her ordeal crashing down on her.

"Don't try to move," Tashi said. Though her own arms were scraped bloody, she attempted to comfort the injured sorceress.

Kaiya's eyes did not miss the fact that her companion was also injured. She placed a hand on the woman's arm, but no magic came. She could not heal the cuts, nor could she provide any comfort for her pain. Accepting her failure, she lay back in the snow and closed her eyes.

Believing the matter to be finished, Tashi allowed the sorceress to rest. Ignoring her own discomfort, she knelt in the snow and stared up at the sky. *We did it, Annin,* she thought. Her niece would be safe. The Gawr would return to sleep. Stretching herself next to Kaiya, she rested her eyes.

Twitching in her sleep, Kaiya saw visions of fire. Malice pierced her heart, the form of a giant haunting her dreams. With one hand it controlled fire, in the other it coerced the wind. The earth rumbled, obeying the whim of the ancient behemoth, the rivers running backward in reply.

Kaiya awoke with a start, her eyes glistening with silver magic. "We have to get back to the mines," she said, hopping to her feet. "Now."

Groggy, Tashi rubbed at her eyes. The two had slept away an entire day. "What's so urgent?" she wondered. The Gawr had been dealt with. Surely now there was time to rest and regain some strength.

"The Gawr is still awake," she said. "It attacked us with that wind."

"How?" Tashi asked, standing. "I thought activating the runes would put it to sleep?"

"They will hold it asleep after I finish the ritual," Kaiya said. "I have to seal the magic against the Gawr, and force it back to its prison."

"And that is in the mines?" Tashi asked.

"It's as deep as I can go," Kaiya replied. "That means it's as close to the Gawr as I can get."

Nodding, Tashi asked, "And this has to be done each cycle?" How could the Ulihi have fought off this terrible creature in the past? Would they be able to fight it in the future?

"No," the sorceress replied. "As long as the runes are kept active, no one will have to face it again." *Assuming I survive the encounter,* she added silently.

"The runes will have weakened it for you,right?" Tashi asked.

"I think activating the runes has made it desperate," Kaiya replied. By renewing the ancient magic, she had forced the Gawr's hand. Now it would fight harder, making a last stand to protect its freedom. This would be the fight of her life.

Chapter 19

Escorted by a blustery wind, the travelers made a final push for the mines. Tashi's knowledge of the area proved invaluable, leading them along unseen paths. Her shortcuts often resulted in treacherous travel over uneven ground, but still they journeyed on. After two days without a pause, they succumbed to fatigue and sat with their backs against boulders, weathered smooth through the millennia.

Neither managed to sleep, the gravity of their task forbidding it. Instead, they sat for an hour, catching their breath and massaging their aching feet.

"Do you believe your village is safe?" Kaiya asked. Ulihi architecture was primitive, far inferior to dwarven construction. Could the village have survived the Gawr's onslaught?

"Yes," Tashi replied with confidence. "We build in sheltered areas. The rockslides will not have affected my people." The Ulihi had lived among these mountains since time began. If the situation grew dire, they would simply migrate to another settlement. They would survive.

Wishing she could be as certain as Tashi, Kaiya's thoughts turned to the question she had feared to ask. Projecting her mind to the wind, she asked, *Does my family still live?* Not an answer, but an image flashed before her eyes. The farmhouse stood, untouched by the destruction that had visited the mining settlement. Her brothers worked the fields, her mother sat on the porch with Flip perched proudly on her lap. Her father puffed his pipe, a blanket draped over his legs. Doozle snoozed at his feet. All was as it should be, as if the Gawr had no effect on her home. *Thank you*, she said to the wind.

Her eyes wet, she slowly pulled herself back to her feet. It was time to face her enemy, to be rid of it before it could damage the one place dearest to her—

before it could crush her already troubled spirit. It was time for the Gawr to slumber once more.

By the following morning, the pair stood within sight of the settlement, the silence of the city overwhelming. Before their eyes, they witnessed the devastation wrought by the Gawr's wrath. Buildings were leveled, entire streets buried beneath piles of mud and stone. It was far worse than they had seen from above.

Kaiya's heart nearly stopped as she looked upon something newly constructed, a cemetery complete with freshly chiseled headstones. These were her kinsmen, dying at the hands of an angry monster. She bowed her head, her eyes stinging.

"Too many have been lost," Tashi whispered, her hand placed over her heart. Guilt rose in her, her stomach clenching. Fighting back the urge to be sick, she renewed her vow to see this through to the end. Though she alone could not finish this. It had to be Kaiya, for Tashi lacked the power. "You must get to the mines," she said, gently patting the dwarf's back.

Lifting her head, Kaiya's throat tightened. Could Galen be among the dead? He had made it through the earlier avalanche, but what might have befallen him after she activated the third rune? The Gawr knew her power, and it could see her mind. Those she loved would not remain safe, if indeed they truly were.

Clenching her teeth, she made up her mind. There was no time to search for Galen. She would have to trust in the wind. Her eyes searched the vicinity for a way to the mine, anything capable of bearing her faster than her own legs. There, munching grass as if the world's evil had no effect on him, stood a bighorn.

Running toward the creature, she jumped onto its back and dug her heels into its flank. The bighorn obeyed, spitting out a mouthful of greens and bleating. Nimbly it climbed over the rubble, its powerful legs unhindered by the mountainside. Higher it went, never slowing, bearing the sorceress to her destination. It stopped outside the mine's entrance and stamped the ground with a forefoot.

Patting its neck, Kaiya thanked the creature for its assistance. Though she did not look behind her, she could feel Tashi's desire to join her. The priestess was coming, though she could not run as fast as the bighorn. With her mind, she reached out to her companion. *Don't follow,* she instructed her. *Remain outside the mine, no matter what you hear. If I don't survive, find Galen and get help from the elves.*

Not waiting for a reply, Kaiya took a deep breath and stepped inside the mine. A sense of dread slammed into her chest. The Gawr's power had grown. Darkness enveloped the sorceress, the only sound the hammering of her heart. One glance at the entryway mirror revealed its destruction. She would have to find her way in the absence of all light.

Her fingers shook, her feet lead weights. *You will get only one chance,* she reminded herself. The absolute stillness of the mine would not allow her magic stores to replenish. She would have to be quick and efficient.

Through great effort, she steadied her breathing, but each breath was too hot and her throat was too dry. *You can do this,* she tried to convince herself as she clenched and relaxed her hands. At the first platform she fidgeted with the rope, tangling it. With shaking fingers, she managed to work it out and descended deeper into the mine. A rumbling echoed through the expansive cavern, reminding her that her enemy was not yet asleep.

Chunks of rock worked their way loose from the ceiling, crashing to the bottom of the mine. One struck the platform, sending it careening toward the next level. Kaiya landed hard, the wind forced from her lungs. As she attempted to pull herself up, she could not. Her leg was pinned beneath the fallen rubble, and she lacked the physical strength to lift it. Trapped in the darkness, she considered her options. Was this worth the magic she would have to spend to free herself? Would she then have enough to face the Gawr? Groaning in frustration, she lay back in the darkness.

* * * * *

"Was that Kaiya?" Daro asked, jogging toward the mine's entrance.

"It was," Tashi replied. Though she had arrived too late to see Kaiya enter, she had no doubt the sorceress had made it to her destination.

"What's she doing? Did you find all those rune stones?"

"We did," the priestess replied. "She has to go deep to seal the magic."

As she finished speaking, the ground shook, sending both of them to their hands and knees. A cry of alarm echoed from inside the mine. Splintering wood announced the destruction of the elevator platform.

"She's in trouble," Daro said. He took a step toward the entrance, but Tashi grabbed his arm.

"She warned me not to follow," the priestess said. "It is too dangerous."

The echo of falling rock, and the groan of an obviously injured woman sounded from the mine, stabbing Tashi through the heart. "She's hurt," she said. "I'll go after her."

"That platform's gone," Daro said. "Let me climb down." The Ulihi woman was slight of build, and the foreman believed himself far sturdier. Her thin arms would never see her safely to the bottom.

"No," Tashi said. "I'm lighter. You can lower me with a rope."

Daro agreed, fetching a length of rope from a nearby crate. Fashioning a makeshift harness, he stepped inside the mine.

Affixing the harness around herself, Tashi tugged at the rope. It felt sturdy. "Fetch your men and wait at the top for us," she told him. "We might need your help, so keep your ears open."

The foreman nodded and lowered the priestess over the ledge. Ignoring the discomfort of the rope, Tashi descended into the vast emptiness. When her feet struck the bottom, she did not hesitate. Freeing herself from the rope, she stumbled into the darkness, her eyes slowly adjusting to the gloom.

Hearing footsteps, Kaiya propped herself up on her elbow. "Who's there?" she called.

"Tashi," the priestess replied, moving toward the voice. Dropping to her knees, she reached for her companion.

"My leg is pinned," Kaiya said, a note of shame in her voice. Her magic could have blasted her free, but she hesitated to use it.

Using her staff as a lever against the rubble, Tashi gave her friend the room she needed to wiggle free.

"Thanks," Kaiya said. With a sigh of relief, she admitted, "I'm glad you came." Here in the dreary underworld, it was comforting to see a familiar face. She had dismissed Tashi too quickly, and she regretted it. The priestess had proved herself invaluable, and her presence might mean the difference between success and failure since it allowed Kaiya to preserve her magic.

A sharp pain shot through Kaiya's leg when she tried to stand. "Ah!" she cried as she nearly fell. Luckily, Tashi was there to catch her. Leaning some of her weight against Tashi, Kaiya attempted to walk through the pain.

The movement did Kaiya some good, and by the time they reached the second platform, she was able to walk on her own. Down they went, Tashi working the ropes to lower themselves with ease. Only the creaking of the platform could be heard, the light fading into complete darkness.

Blindly they moved on, trusting their feet to follow the path. Disorientation swept over them, but they reached for each other in the dark, steadying themselves whenever needed. The third platform awaited, a gentle rolling thunder sounding beneath it.

"Are you sure you don't want to turn back?" Kaiya asked. Tashi had no magic to protect herself, and Kaiya would not be able to spare any to shield her. The priestess had already done enough. Without her, Kaiya wouldn't have made it this far without using magic.

"I am with you until the end," Tashi declared. Grasping the ropes, she lowered the platform, her eyes fixated on the glowing green dots of light. *Such beautiful creatures hidden from the world,* she thought. "Do those creatures use magic?" she asked.

The true source of their light was unknown to her, but Kaiya sensed no magic in the glowworms. Though she couldn't see her friend's face, she could sense the wonder in her voice. Rather than dash her spirits, she replied, "I don't know, but if they have magic, let's hope they use it to aid us."

"I think they already have," the priestess replied. The mere presence of such beauty reassured her that evil could not taint every inch of the world. Even here, where the dead god's wrath was strongest, it could not thwart the magic of these tiny beings.

Setting foot on the lowest level, both women could feel the presence of evil. A faint red glow appeared in the distance, near the end of the mine where Kaiya had stood before. Unable to spend magic on light, the sorceress did her best to guide her companion from memory. The earth groaned its dissatisfaction as they reached the mine's end.

Flattening herself on the cold floor, Kaiya's eyes burned with silver magic. Spreading her hands flat on the stone, she focused her mind to the spell that would seal the Gawr to its prison. Tashi recoiled at the sight of the magic burning at her feet, the sudden illumination painful to her eyes.

As the magic spread, the ground rumbled. Steady at first, it crescendoed to a deafening roar, forcing the priestess to cover her ears. The vibrations resonated throughout her body, her teeth chattering and head throbbing. Concerned that the sorceress would be forced to abandon the spell, she kneeled at her side, but Kaiya showed no sign that she was affected. Her years of practice with meditation made her focus difficult to break, despite the Gawr's efforts.

Silver light stretched along the cavern floor, extending itself into the walls. Tiny deposits of painite glowed red in response. Tashi saw them as bleeding hearts, the lifeblood of her people and the dwarves. Lives would be saved, or all would end here. Though she had no magic, she projected a powerful message to the dead god. *Sleep, evil, and leave the world in peace.*

Her mind in close proximity to the Gawr, Kaiya could feel its power. It was far stronger than before, its will to destroy greater than ever. With all its being, it fought her, attempting to break through her spell. The ground shook, knocking loose chunks of rock and opening fissures in the floor. Still the sorceress held fast. If she lost her concentration, she wouldn't have the power to start over. With no wind available to her, the air could not be replenished, nor could her magical stores. This had to work.

With an earsplitting crash, three fractures appeared in the walls nearest the sorceress. Though dizzy from the constant rumbling, Tashi steeled her courage. Through the openings emerged three stone beasts, each stumbling on four legs. Despite their clumsy movements, they closed in on Kaiya, who refused to drop her spell to deal with them. All she needed was a few more minutes.

Tashi would give them to her. Reaching for an abandoned mining pick, she gripped it tightly in her hands. Swinging with all her might, she attacked the nearest stone beast, sending rocks flying. Spurred on by her success, she hacked away, focusing on its legs to render it immobile. Without pause, she moved on, swinging her pick at the second beast. Forcing it away from Kaiya, she hacked at its feet, which were little more than a jumbled pile of rock. *You should have built a better monster,* she wanted to say to the Gawr.

The floor quaked, shaking the entire cavern violently. Midswing, Tashi had no time to steady herself. Her awkward position left her top-heavy, and she plummeted to the ground, striking her hip and shouting out in pain. Seeing an opportunity to rid itself of a threat, the third stone beast closed in on her.

Thanks to the light of Kaiya's magic, Tashi saw her attacker drawing near. It kicked out with a massive leg, but she rolled to her left, avoiding the blow. Still on the ground, she found her way to a seated position before striking again. The pick swiped the beast's foot from beneath it, sending it staggering backward. Not wasting a moment, she found her feet and lunged at the beast, bringing the pick down on top of its head. It shrunk back, giving her the opportunity she needed. Putting all her energy into one swing, she smashed through one leg and then the other three. It fell, wriggling on its torso, no longer a threat.

Still lying on the floor, Kaiya's brow glistened with sweat. Her muscles ached, an explosion of pain in her head threatening to break what focus she had left. It was all too much, and the fear of failure worked its way into her mind.

The Gawr's power was beginning to fade, she could feel it in her bones. But her own magic was dwindling, and she would soon be forced into submission. Both she and the Gawr had much to lose, and neither would give up willingly.

In one last effort, she drew on the small amount of air that remained in the cavern. The room glowed brighter as the breath escaped the sorceress's lungs, the pressure in her chest excruciating. The Gawr responded with an earsplitting cry, the cavern walls crumbling and collapsing, the ceiling raining down.

Dizzy from the lack of air and overexertion, Tashi felt herself fading. The room spun before her eyes, the quaking ground only adding to her disorientation. Blackness crept around the edges of her vision. The last sight she saw was a stone beast limping its way toward her. Crumpling to the ground, she saw no more.

Falling stones pelted Kaiya as she desperately fought to stay conscious. As the darkness crept over her, she knew she had failed. She could not hold the spell any longer. The Dwarf's Heart trapped within the mine's walls glowed brighter, filling her final vision with images of red, the blood of those she could not save.

A searing heat scorched her skin through the pocket of her tunic, a new source of magic announcing itself. *Galen's rune!* Kaiya remembered, her hand desperately reaching for the source of power. It glimmered in the silver light, a red flame on its surface. Pulling its energy through herself, she revitalized her magical stores and commanded the rune to obey.

A blast of wind swept through the cavern, reviving the fallen priestess and shattering the rock beasts as they attempted to flee. Momentarily refreshed, Kaiya marveled at the elf's power. *He's not much of a sorcerer, but he's a damn fine rune carver,* she mused. Refocusing her energy, she renewed the spell that would seal her enemy to its fate.

A growl of displeasure sounded from the Gawr, the image of a gigantic hand lashing out playing over in Kaiya's mind. With a burst of anger, the beast called down its final attack, rocking the mine at its foundation.

Groggy and unsteady on her feet, Tashi watched as the sorceress completed her spell. The entire cavern shook in defiance, a tremendous growl reverberating throughout. In a flash of silver light, Tashi felt the mine's floor collapse, sending them plummeting deeper into the earth.

A pile of stones collapsed on Tashi, crushing the small bones of one foot. One struck her directly in the chest, sending an explosion of pain into her throat. Scraped and battered, she was forced to crawl, making every effort to reach the sorceress who had landed face down on the rocks.

Kaiya's head struck the rocks beneath her, knocking her unconscious. The silver light faded, her sealing spell broken. Clutched in her hand, the rune stone faded out, its fire completely spent.

Chapter 20

Stumbling in the darkness, Tashi did her best to find Kaiya among the rubble. All was silent, the cries of distress from beneath dissipating as the ancient monster was forced back to its slumber. The dead god had returned to its rightful place. Her soul was now wiped clean, thanks to Kaiya. Grateful to her friend, the priestess was determined to get to her.

Only the tiny lights put off by the glowworms allowed Tashi to locate her companion. The sorceress did not move, but she still drew breath. Mustering her strength, the priestess pulled her companion along the rubble, hoping to find a way back up. Her every breath labored, the process proved almost too much. Her own body was badly injured, a hot, wet pain in her

lungs. The exertion forced her to cough, leaving the taste of blood heavy in her mouth.

The pair had fallen into a deep chasm, nearly a hundred feet lower than the mine's lowest platform. Tashi limped backward, dragging her friend along the uneven floor, hoping for a miracle. When she crashed into an unseen wall and stumbled backward, she realized she had found one.

Dots of green light illuminated the wall, allowing her to make out what she had found. Stretching out her arms, she examined the area behind her. The debris had collapsed in a funnel shape, creating a makeshift staircase of jumbled rock. The journey up would be awkward, but it was a way out.

Struggling under the sorceress's weight, Tashi forced herself to pull harder. More coughing followed by more blood, the pain in her chest growing more intense. It spread through her body, each breath becoming more difficult. Ignoring the pain, she climbed higher, still dragging Kaiya along with her. Desperately hoping her companion would wake, she wondered how much longer she could continue to pull her. It was more than her injured body could handle.

One final obstacle lay ahead as she neared the mine's platform. A gap of four feet, taller than the priestess, remained for her to climb. Lifting Kaiya to such height would be impossible. She could not lift the sorceress over her head.

Leaving Kaiya on the upper step, Tashi descended and began piling smaller rocks to craft a makeshift ramp. The work was difficult, made more so by her inability to take a full breath. Panting heavily and aching with fatigue, she finished her task and dragged the sorceress upward. Rolling her limp body onto the platform, Tashi reached for the ropes and began to pull. The platform did not move. Her arms lacked the strength to lift both women to the next level.

Removing herself from the platform, Tashi tried again. With only Kaiya to lift, the platform began to move, though slowly. Her eyes glistened as she strained to see her companion rising toward freedom. When Kaiya had safely reached the second plateau, Tashi tied off the rope and lay back, blood pouring from her mouth. Each cough forced more air from her lungs, the blood replacing it in a steady flow.

A light appeared before Tashi's eyes, a torch moving toward her from the darkness. Her mouth dropped open as she realized who had come. Annin stood before her, her eyes gleaming in the darkness.

"Sister," Tashi whispered, reaching out her hands.

Annin took her sister's hands in her own.

"I thought you would hate me," Tashi whispered.

"Never," Annin replied.

Tashi breathed a sigh of relief.

"Come with me," Annin said. "Together we shall be at peace in the world to come."

"But your daughter," Tashi protested. Someone had to protect the girl and train her to fulfill her destiny.

"We will watch over her together," Annin said. Looking upward, she added, "The life you have saved will protect her as well. And she will train her in the use of magic."

Her heart swelling with pride, Tashi smiled. All she could have hoped for would come to pass. Evil had been banished, and her niece would grow to be the protector of the Ulihi. Silently she closed her eyes and slept.

* * * * *

"I'm going down there," Raad said. His first attempt had been hindered by Daro, who feared a massive cave-in would trap any miner who went down. Raad no longer cared. He couldn't stand by while lives were lost.

Grabbing a torch and lighting it, he motioned for the others to follow. In truth, he cared not if they obeyed. His eyes adjusting to the darkness, he tuned his ears to the sound of a pulley. "Hurry," he shouted to the others.

One by one, six dwarves fitted themselves with ropes and were lowered to the second plateau. As they raced through the cavern, embers falling from their torches, they encountered no resistance. The ground no longer shook, no rocks fell from the ceiling, and no thundering could be heard from beneath.

"There!" Raad said, pointing toward the platform. It came to a halt as the miners approached, a single figure lay unmoving. "It's the sorceress," he said, kneeling next to her. Placing his ear near her nose, he said, "She's breathing." With the help of another dwarf, he pulled her from the platform. "Get her out of here," he said. "We'll go and look for Tashi."

The dwarf muscled Kaiya over his shoulder and trotted off into the dark. The others hopped onto the platform and lowered themselves into the deep. Stepping carefully, they made their way over fallen rock. Raad paused when his foot connected with something unseen. Bending down, he lowered his fading torch, the serene face of Tashi illuminated by the pale orange light.

"Oh no," he said as the light revealed her injuries. Blood still trickled out the corners of her mouth, a puddle forming beneath her. "Let's get her to the top," he said, his voice suddenly hoarse. He knew she was gone.

Gently the dwarves lifted her onto the platform and raised it to the top. Raad cradled her in his arms as he was hoisted to the mine's entrance. With tears in his eyes, he looked to Daro and shook his head.

"Put her down here," Daro said quietly.

Raad laid the body on a soft patch of earth and folded her hands across her belly. The dwarves nearby removed their hats and bowed their heads. From the corner of his eye, Raad noticed a tall figure running toward the scene. Word had reached Galen of Kaiya's return.

"Where is she?" he shouted as he reached the mine. Seeing the grim expression on Raad's face, he feared the worst. *Not Kaiya*, he thought, a lump rising in his throat. As he moved closer, he saw both women lying on the ground. Immediately he went to Kaiya's side.

"She's alive," Daro reassured him. "It's the other who didn't make it."

For a moment Galen felt relieved. Then he felt guilty. He looked over at Tashi and closed his eyes. *I'm an ass,* he thought. All he had cared about was Kaiya, but it was Tashi whose life had been lost. Sitting back on his heels, he allowed his tears to fall, tears that Tashi would not want. She had gone home to her sister. "Sleep in peace," he whispered.

Kaiya stirred, a single groan escaping her throat. Her mind reeling, she sat up. "Where's Tashi?" she asked. Her eyes met Galen's, and she knew immediately. Turning her head, she looked upon her fallen companion. "No," she said, scrambling to her feet. Kneeling next to Tashi, she placed both hands over the priestess's heart, silver magic spreading over her body. All life was gone. Kaiya was too late.

Defeated, Kaiya buried her face in her hands and wept. Galen moved to her side and wrapped an arm around her. Squeezing her tightly, he kissed the side of her head.

"She's at peace," he whispered.

"She died saving me," Kaiya said.

"She died for her people," Galen corrected. "This is what she came here to do. You know it as well as I do."

The elf was right. Kaiya's magic had allowed her a glimpse into Tashi's mind. The priestess had met death with dignity, knowing she had completed her mission. Evil would no longer haunt the Ulihi. It was the greatest gift she could give her people. Now she would live for eternity, safe in the arms of her beloved sister. Tashi couldn't ask for anything more wonderful. Her death had not been in vain.

This knowledge gave Kaiya some comfort, but still she wept. Wrapping her arms around Galen, she allowed herself to grieve. Together they mourned the passing of a remarkable woman, a friend to them both.

"What should we do with the body?" Daro asked, his voice soft.

"I'm going to visit the Ulihi," Kaiya replied. "I'll take her home."

"I'll come along," Raad announced. "It'd be an honor to escort Tashi back to her people." He would personally see to it that she was treated with respect.

"Do you think they'll want to be friendly with us after the death of their High Priestess?" Daro asked.

"They will," Kaiya reassured him. "The Gawr has been contained, and their people are safe. It will fall to them to see that it stays that way. The miners must live in peace with the Ulihi."

"You have my word on that," Daro replied.

"You should rest before we leave," Raad said. "It'll take a few hours to get my cart ready anyway. The bighorns need to be fed and watered."

Nodding, Kaiya replied, "We'll leave at first light." Her head was still spinning from her ordeal, though a warm wind gently tousled her hair. The pain in her heart spread throughout her veins with every beat. The wind could do nothing to ease such a wound. "I hope to leave for home after I visit the Ulihi," she said to Galen. "Will you be coming with me?"

The elf paused for a moment. "I think I'll stay here awhile," he finally said. "There's much more I can learn about the Dwarf's Heart. Its magical properties are remarkable."

"They truly are," she replied. "Your rune saved me down there. It gave me the strength I needed to finish the Gawr. Without that rune, I surely would have failed."

"All the more reason for me to finish my studies," the elf replied. He swallowed hard. Being apart from his dearest friend would be difficult. "I'll return with the next caravan heading south. Maybe after that I'll book passage to the Sunswept Isles." There was much he could learn from the elves of the isles with regard to painite.

"Now there's a place I'd love to see," Kaiya said, finding her smile. The idea of sunshine and blue seas would be a welcome change from stone and ice.

"I'd be delighted to have you with me," he said.

"Don't stay away too long," she replied. "It won't feel like home without you."

"Speaking of home," he said. "Do you know if the village still stands? Your family, and Trin, are they safe? And what of the Vale?"

"Everyone is fine," she replied with certainty. "The wind has seen to it."

Reaching out his hand, he helped her to her feet. Still wobbly, she appreciated his help. Rest would not come easy, but exhaustion eventually overcame her. In her dreams she saw Tashi, arm in arm with her sister. A deep feeling of peace washed over her.

* * * * *

As Raad's cart slowly approached the Ulihi village, every member of the tribe paused in their chores. Those who were inside their homes came out to see who had come. Without any announcement, they knew that Tashi was gone. The somber expressions on the faces of the dwarves spoke louder than any word. Most of the tribesmen hung their heads, save for the priestesses who approached the cart.

Setting the brake, Raad tipped his hat to the women. Kaiya hopped down from the cart and spied the doula, Annin's baby clutched tightly in her arms. Tears dripped from the sorceress's eyes, her heart aching for the child's loss. She would know neither her mother nor her aunt, a grave misfortune indeed.

"Tashi has died?" one priestess asked, already knowing the answer.

Kaiya gave a single nod. "She gave her life for my own, and for her people."

"I've brought her home," Raad said, tilting his head toward the cart. Tashi lay lifeless, a small bouquet of yellow flowers placed in her hands. Even in death she was beautiful, her features undiminished.

"We will honor her," the priestess said.

"It now falls to your people to maintain hold over the Gawr," Kaiya said. "I will teach you how to perform the spells to keep the rune stones active."

"None of us have magical talent," the priestess admitted.

"One of you does," she said, gesturing to the baby.

The priestess motioned for the doula to approach. "This child has magic?" she asked.

"She does," Kaiya replied. "The ritual won't need to be performed for a dozen years," she explained. "That will give me time to teach her how to perform the spells. I'll also be visiting with the king to let him know how valuable your people are to us and all of Nōl'Deron."

"You have been of great service to us," the priestess said. "It is most appreciated. I would offer you something in return."

"I couldn't ask for a reward," the sorceress replied. Tashi had already given her life. That was far more than Kaiya felt she deserved.

"There is a ceremony among our people. A bonding, you might call it," the priestess said. "This child has no mother nor aunt. The ceremony would create a bond of sisterhood between you and her."

Choking on her tears, Kaiya managed to say, "It would be an honor beyond words." Even without the ceremony, she felt a depth of affection for the girl. In her short life, she had suffered too much loss.

The doula passed the sleeping infant to Kaiya, who cradled her gently against her chest. Softly she kissed the girl on her forehead, a single tear splashing on her ebony skin. The child awoke, a flash of silver in her eyes.

About the Author

Lana Axe lives in the Missouri countryside surrounded by dogs, cats, birds, and reptiles. She spends most of her free time daydreaming about elves, magic, and faraway lands.

For more information, please visit: <u>lana-axe.com</u>.

www.ingramcontent.com/pod-product-compliance
Lightning Source LLC
Chambersburg PA
CBHW030027180626
46810CB00001B/254